ALCHEMIST OF THE EAST

APORVA KALA

First published in India in 2016 by Muskdeer Publishing

deer.musk@yahoo.in

Copyright © Aporva Kala 2016

ISBN: 9789384439675

Aporva Kala asserts the moral right to be identified as the author of this work.

First Edition

Cover design: Wasim Helal

Publishing facilitation: AuthorsUpFront

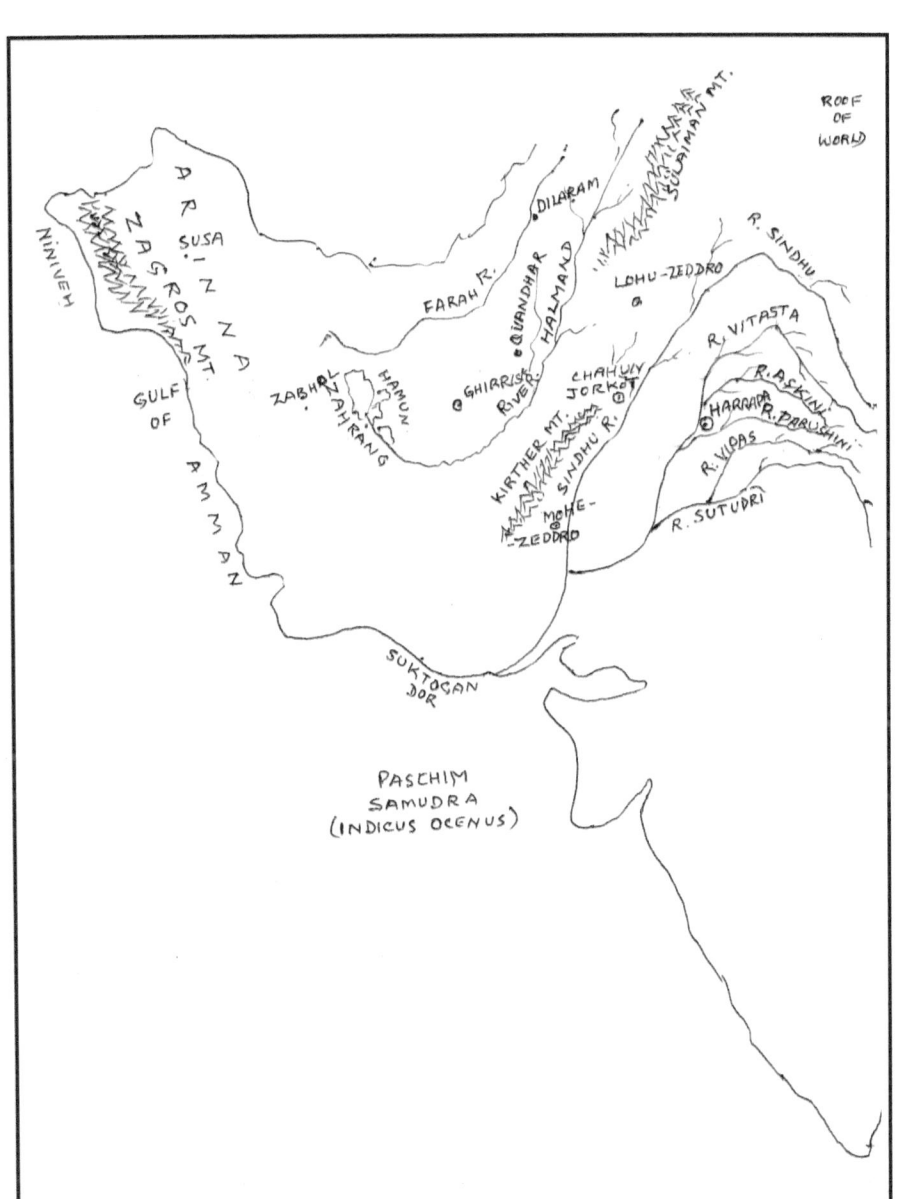

Content

Prologue

"Do you want to know how it all began?" the old man asked.

The Alchemist nodded, her long hair waving in the late evening gale.

"Before the creation of this world, the world we live in, there were the Gods who lived in a beautiful place called Dev Lok – the abode of the Gods. There were no deaths, no nights and a never ending day of peace, prosperity, and happiness prevailed. In this world were born the twins Yama and Yami, the brother sister duo, through the Sun-god, to the couple Vivasvant and Saranyu. Soon the twins were everybody's favourites and were the cause of immense pleasure to the residents of Dev Lok. They grew under the watchful eyes of Agni, Varuna and Brahspati."

The Alchemist shifted uneasily and looked towards the blue waters of the river Parushini which reflected the red ball of the setting sun.

"Be patient," the old man said. "I am coming to the essence of this legend. The twins were young and beautiful as they entered the age of adolescence. Yama preferred to stay in the forests, near the water bodies and listen to the flute. Yami was extremely attached to her brother. One day when Yama was resting near a lake, Yami saw him and was charmed by her own brother. It was spring time and the flowers were in full bloom while the insects played humming tunes. It was at this very moment the arrow of Kama, the god of love and copulation struck Yami. Her passion rose and sought their consummation through Yama. But Yama rebuked her and asked her to find another soul mate for herself. We have to live a life of values and morality, he claimed. But Yami wouldn't budge from her demand of marrying her own brother. Through a rigorous exposition of logic and reason, Yama was able to douse the fire of passions of his sister. It was he who expounded the first tenets of ethics for humanity," the old man paused for a while.

"What does it prove? What did Yama have in mind?" the Alchemist asked.

"That we humans should have a high degree of moral values; but wait, I haven't finished as yet. Now it happened that Yama was destined to die and his was the path of death. One day Yami found Yama lying on a huge stone slab. He wouldn't wake up. Soon the gods declared him dead. But Yami was blinded by grief and cried incessantly, telling everyone that her brother had died today. Remember there were no nights then. Yami's crying caused huge floods and fire broke out in many a places. Doomsday was around the corner. The Gods were a worried lot and called a hurried meeting. It was decided that night be created so that Yami would believe that her brother had died the day before. Soon night was created and Yami told everyone that her brother had died the day before. Slowly her grief diminished," the old man paused.

"This is how the lovely nights and the shiny stars came into being?" the Alchemist asked.

"Indeed, but I haven't finished as yet. Yama was the first mortal and it was he who made it possible for us mortals to die and seek salvation in the God's abode – Heaven. It is he who presides over the good and the bad deeds of us humans and he is the supreme judge allocating hell or heaven to the dead according to their karmas."

"He is our first ancestor, then?" the Alchemist asked.

"Yes, Yama and Yami were the first couple who brought progeny on this earth. They are the first parents of the world." The old man stood up slowly.

"Now Yama rules the abode of our ancestors and takes the dead on the journey to the other world. He is assisted by two four-eyed dogs and has an owl and a pigeon as his messengers. As for Yami, her tears came to earth in the form of the river Yamuna, which is why it is said that a mere dip into the holy waters of the Yamuna removes the fear of death."

"So is this how humanity started?" the Alchemist reflected.

"Yes, but now we have a world full of evil, animosity, wars, jealously, discord and...."

"But there is goodness, too," the Alchemist interrupted the old man. "We worship the gods, make offerings to the lords, practice charity, say our daily prayers and seek to chase our dreams."

"Yes...yes... we should have faith in the eternal goodness of human beings. And then there are the likes of you, the *shakti*, who give the mortals, the power to realise their destiny."

"Yes, everybody has it in them to become what they want to. One can be one's hero, one's personal God." the Alchemist said as she bid him goodbye.

Journey to Melhua

THE GLORY OF THE Assyrian rule over Mesopotamia, which had reached its zenith under the leadership of Emperor Tigleth Pileser, had been brought to an ignominious end by the marauding tribes from North Africa, the Caucasus Mountains, the Balkans and those from Mount Urartu near Lake Van.

The Dark Age of civilisations had well and truly set in.

However, during that period a ray of hope shone in the form of two great holy scriptures: the *Avesta* and the *Rig Veda*.

Situated on the banks of the river Tigris, Nineveh, the Mesopotamian capital, was encircled by the remains of the great wall of the state of Mesopotamia that had baked bricks sprayed across the river bank forming an embankment of sorts. A few of these large bricks lay like tombstones on the shallow banks of the river while some lay like isolated islands; in heaps forming huge mounds which the Ninevehians called the seats of wisdom. Why had they named them thus was not known, but these mounds, of them there were several, had become the part of the legend of the dying city, which lay in ruins. The fallen wall symbolised present day annihilation as much as it reminded one of the glorious past; a past of prosperity and peace, of arts and literature, of music and dance, of prayers in the fire temples and of the worship of Goddess Ishtar.

One morning, on the banks of this mighty river, a red-haired young boy sat on one of the square mounds of the splayed bricks, wondering about history of which he wasn't a part, but which, for him held a mysterious pull – a magical weave of the most joyous type. He could almost imagine the artists meditating upon beautiful engravings on the baked bricks and terracotta seals and the musicians playing the harp or the banjo. It would have been a life of peace, bliss and plenty he concluded. He regretted the unleashing of violence by fellow tribesmen, for he considered all the tribes, of them there were innumerable hordes, to be one big family. Now his lovely city lay under the depths of hunger and squalor, where death lurked in every nook and corner. The citizens fearful of any eventuality that might occur, had surrendered to the charms of all things evil and lived a life of utter moral turpitude.

Sushyo, as the seventeen year old boy was known as, sat with a grim demeanor, wondering how he, if left free to make toys, could bring peace and happiness to the citizens of the dying city.

"Toys are the mirrors of the heart," he mumbled, "One day, I will make toys which will bring a smile on the faces of even the most dejected lot."

The boy ignored the barbs of his fellow men and wore his ambition with a resolve of a winner. Presently, he jumped from the brick mound, arranged his green cotton tunic and a red dotted head gear, pulled out a sling from his waistband and arranged a round stone on the sling's goatskin headed belt. He aimed at the river waters, pulled the strap and released it with a jerk. The stone flew with a swirl and danced over the waters several times before immersing in the squalid waters of the river.

"Seven!" he shouted gaily.

He hurried through the dull bazaars where few buyers jostled with fewer sellers. The tribal warriors stood in vigil, policing the meager goods that lay in the shops.

Bad times don't end on their own, the boy thought and ran the full distance of the narrow streets when he was accosted by Nirroon, his uncle; a shabby, shaky man with a humped back weighing his carcass down.

"Hey son, stop and give the old man some support, I can't walk much now. There is the fear of attack by the thugs from the hills and across the rivers which keeps me indoors. Good I met you. Come hurry up, we have to go to the souk for vegetables and oil. Your mother has asked me to bring the things as she is cooking something special," he caught the boy's fluttering tunic and spoke in a harsh tone.

"I have to bake a few of my toys; later the sun will be too hot. Let me go," the boy countered with a soft whisper as he struggled to free himself from his uncle's grip.

"What toys-voys? Get on with life, boy. At your age I was married and had a few kids, a family to feed while you wander like a useless cad. No way will I let you live the life of a spoilt brat. Come along and help me carry out your mother's orders," Nirroon hissed.

The boy kicked the earth and held on to his uncle' limp body, almost carrying him. They bought a ripe pumpkin and a few drumsticks. The boy walked sulkily back to his house listening to his uncle's rant about the youth going awry and shying away from their natural responsibilities, of living life according to the seasons and begetting as many children as they could.

"Uncle I am going to be a toy maker and I will trade my toys with the Greeks and the rulers of Anatolia. I will be rich and will marry a girl from the Himalayas, I have heard they are beautiful and fair...." his voice trailed him.

No sooner had he placed the vegetables in the kitchen and gone to his backyard to lay his freshly designed toys to dry under the sun that there was a loud explosion. A devastating fire broke out through the row of hay huts and dark brooding smoke engulfed the city. The people who survived went about saving the ones they could, as if it were a matter of routine for them.

For the boy, however, all was lost. His parents had been devoured by the fire goddess. The boy's faith in Lord Ahura on whom his mother showered her devotion, was shaken. There is I and then there is God, he thought. I have to be up to it to do things on my own. No Ahura will come to help me in my time of distress, he concluded.

Yet, he couldn't forget the pain of losing his parents and grieved for days. His face grew pale and his eyes sunk deep into the holes. With a haggard look he roamed about the empty streets of Nineveh, pleading with whomsoever he laid his eye on, to search for his parents. He made little figurines of clay and carried them close to his chest, claiming them to be those of his father and mother.

One day, in his delirious misery the boy had wandered deep into the desert and lay on the warm sands, clinging on to his last breath. An old man came across him, whose age few knew, and with the help of his ardent followers picked up the limp body of the boy. He nursed the boy to health in his sailboat which had dropped anchor on the banks of river Tigris.

Soon they took to the seas and the old man, who was the Captain and was called thus by everyone had only the right eye to see. Over his left eye he wore a black band. He chose to put the boy, who now had recuperated, in charge of rowing the sailboat.

The boy was repulsed by the idea of forever being thrown into the muck of slavery, and pleaded that he should be put to some skilled work for he was a creative soul who needed all the encouragement. He could provide that one thing which the humans need to survive – to be happy and to breathe freely.

"And what, may I ask, is that thing that you promise to provide?" the Captain grinned as if he were playing with his hunt before the kill.

"*The beauty of the soul and the simplicity of happiness,*" the boy replied in a poetic tone which attracted the burly pirate-like band of sea-men.

"It is important to be in tune with the happiness within," the boy said. "My mother had always told me to be the cause of other's happiness."

"Is that possible? To be happy and all the farcical truths?" One of the Captain's men asked.

"Yes indeed, look at me,' the boy continued, 'I was as good as dead when my mother's *rooh* or her spirit came and saved me and told me that my work was to spread smiles on earth."

"And how do you intend to carry on with...ughh... er... spreading smiles across the globe?" the bawdy crowd chorused sarcastically.

"By making toys," the boy said with a calm dignity. "Toys are man's best friends."

"Hah.... Well, toy-maker, when I picked you up from the dreadful desert you were as good as dead, with a horde of vultures keen to nibble on whatever flesh remained on your carcass. So, it happens, dear boy, that I am your saviour and hence you owe me a favour for all the meals I feed you and of course for saving you from certain death," the Captain claimed haughtily.

"Was I dead?" the boy asked. "How did I reach the river bank? I was... and... and... who are you all?" The boy stopped rowing and surveyed his surroundings with a sense of helpless despondency.

"I don't know who brought you to the river bank, but I know, and I know it for a fact, that if you are alive, it is nothing short of a miracle," the Captain mocked.

"Thank Mehraj for saving you, for it was he who insisted on bringing you to this sailboat."

"Yes, the Captain speaks the truth. You were dead, but you were brought back by the herbal broth of Annarria, our head cook, who fed you life-saving liquids through a bamboo pipe thrust down your throat." A tall bearded man added. "Indeed you owe us your life, Sonny, we are your saviours."

"I don't know how I reached the vast desert as I lost my consciousness after my mother....oh... how I miss her..." the boy wailed as he remembered the death of his parents.

"You say you found me and my bag... did you find my bag? Where is it?" the boy asked as he struggled to get up and free himself from the heavy oars which were chained to his wrists.

"It lay beside you when we found you among the ruins of the ill-fated wall at the mouth of the desert." the Captain clarified. "What does it contain? King Solomon's treasure?" he laughed hoarsely.

"More than all the treasures of the whole wide world of yours, Captain. It contains my dream which I am keen to make my destiny. My mother..." tears rolled down the boy's swollen eyes.

"So, here we have one more of the tribe who dreams... haha. Good one young boy. At your age one can, but once you wake up to reality you will find that you belong to the category of slaves. But I will be fair with you. Once we reach the ports of Suktangot Dor in the lands of Melhua, I will set you free and even help you get immigration clearance if you need it; that of course comes with a condition: if we are able to complete our voyage before our sailboat capsizes."

By now a crowd of sorts had gathered around the hull of the

boat and the fellow rowers had stopped rowing, keen to listen to the tale of the boy's adventures.

"I add to your numbers, and in these times of distress and trouble, an extra hand is a welcome addition; that the dear Captain of the seven seas explains your benevolence towards me but now it seems I have fallen into the hands of a bunch of pirates." the boy knew he had to use all his ingenuity and guile to save his skin.

"Of course we are short of men. But rowing would do you a world of good. In a few days you will have a calm mind and a muscular body. You see, boy, an ungratified appetite, and performing the deed one dislikes is the best exercise. Hence, I have assigned you the position of an oarsman on this ship," the Captain jeered.

"But rest assured and I give you my word that we are no pirates but freedom fighters."

"A ship!" the boy cried, "this boat or whatever the ugly piece of wood might disintegrate any time now."

The Captain stared hard at him.

He was an old man of many seasons with long silver hair and carried a scimitar, engraved with strange faces and figures. A gold brocaded robe, which had lost its shine but not its dignity, hung loosely on his frail figure. From the battle scared face, his right eye shone like the morning star while a black band covered his left eye.

The Captain stood up from the wooden plank on which he sat like a king and caught hold of the dangling rope to climb up to the boat's floor.

"Hey…Captain..free me and I will prove that I have much more than a mere slave in your boat; I believe in my skill and art and I can repair your… er… brig… ship… or whatever," the boy challenged him.

The Captain continued his climb up to the deck, leaving the boy in the dark dingy hold of the boat. His loyal followers followed him.

"Meer, should we free him or..?" he asked.

"We do need a clown on this ship; the boy is a natural story-teller; a good comic relief for our men," Meer grinned.

"Ah... hmm....."

The boy has guts, the Captain thought and he has an instinct for survival, like a well bred. He was as good as gone lying under the killing sun, for god knows how many days and yet he hung on to life. The *Rooh* was none other than Lord Ahura Mazada.

He rushed back to the brig's hold and shouted. "Hey boy, that day Lord Ahura himself visited you through the *Rooh* and saved your life. Now pray and remember your destiny is to be a slave and no more. Toy-maker, rowing is your destiny and to be my slave, your fate."

"If it was *he*, who saved me through a *Rooh*, then be assured I will make my own destiny by following my dreams. I am blessed by *him*, of whom you talk with such praise and piety," the boy shouted back. "And Captain, the *Rooh* was none other than my mother; she is the god I believe in and not on your Ahura..."

The sobs of the boy echoed through the sailboat.

But deep down the boy knew that he would have to use all his common sense to get out of the mess he had unknowingly landed himself in. It was good the sailboat was sailing to the lands of Melhua. Sheer luck! But what if it capsized before reaching the ports?

His sixth sense warded the greater dangers of Gueitean pirates who run amuck in the gulf and on the waters of the *Oceanus Indicus*. Or it would be the high tides, making it tough to navigate. He wiped his tears and pulled out his bag and struggled to empty it on the floor of the ship. A fellow oarsman helped him. He surveyed its contents – a few round stones, a box of cotton string and sewing needles, a chiseler, some other tiny tools gifted by his father, an amulet, his sling, a few dried figs, dates and almonds and a notebook. He flipped through its pages and stark empty white sheets glared at him. Oh Mother! Tears filled up his innocent eyes as he mumbled a prayer and then wore the amulet around his neck.

'And, dear Captain, the *Rooh* of my mother who had come to save me when I lay dead, would come again to save me from your clutches,' the boy mumbled in his anguish.

Old man, you are wrong, one day I will be a great toy-maker, he vowed; his mind working up one solution after another till he reached the one which he was looking for. He kissed the amulet and closed his eyes in a silent prayer to his mother. The boy knew that his problems gave him the reason to escape and follow his destiny; he was surprised that he thought about his destiny to escape from his present predicament. It was only the second time he had surprised himself. The first time was when he had resisted throwing himself into the fire that had devoured his parents.

The sailboat was called *Gilgamesh*. A blue flag with imprints of a peepul tree and a peacock fluttered on its masthead. It sailed rather smoothly on the swift waters of the river Tigris, reaching Bussrah where the rapids of the river Euphrates joined the calm waters of river Tigris.

The boy was pleasantly surprised at the navigability of the boat as it docked at the port of Bussrah. It meant freedom from continuous rowing; he looked at his palms in dismay. They were swollen and the skin had ruptured at a few places. Fellow oarsmen hurried on, whistling in delight at having reached land without capsizing. Travel is the best form of forgetting and forgiving, boy, somebody from the motley group proclaimed, providing a soothing balm to the boy's homesickness. Ah! So true, he thought, why hadn't I thought of it while my mother was alive?

The boy had never been thus far from his city and so enjoyed the freedom that comes from floating on waters of unknown places. New places give wings to one's dreams and turn grief into a tamable feeling. The old Captain was kind enough to let his group of men to take a break. Keen to explore the port town, the boy accompanied them to the streets of Bussrah.

Meanwhile the captain stocked the boat with provisions; warning the crew of the dangers of scarcity once they enter the gulf of Amman. A ship engineer was called upon to give his verdict on the boat's ability to sail through the gulf and into the *Indicus Oceanus*. On seeing the multiple leaks in the boat's hull and a tattered mainmast, he gave a loud cry, much to the dismay of the captain. He promptly shunted the poor engineer off proclaiming that the sailboat was the healthiest that he has set sail in and that within a few full moon days it would dock in the port of Suktangot Dor, in the lands of Melhua.

But the boy knew how fragile the ship was; decaying wooden planks, torn sails and a leak at the stern posed a threat to its sailing. It could sink anytime, the boy thought as he went about examining the large boat. But it hadn't, at least till they navigated the swift waters of the Tigris! His pleas on repair work fell on the Captain's deaf years. We have to hurry our journey, young man, this isn't your trip of leisure, he warned and the boat set sail without repairs. The boy cursed his luck as he rowed to the beats of a drummer, who directed the oarsmen's rowing speed.

Dhak... Dhak... Dhak... Dhuk... Dhak... Dhak... Dhak... Dhuk...

On a starless, moonless day, with black clouds guarding the sky; *Gilgamesh* lost its main sails under a gush of heavy north winds. The bamboo mast, which carried it, broke into two. It rendered sailing a difficult task, though the smaller sail, the mizzen, held on. Yet the boat was at the mercy of huge waves. A concerned captain paced up and down the deck, mumbling prayers and eyeing a few cracked ores which added to his misery.

The boy though, smelled his opportunity; *finding solutions in times of distress makes a hero of a man;* he remembered his mother's words.

He smiled and rowed with a new found vigour. Let the high tide wane, and then dear captain, we will see who the real man of the seven seas is.

The next day, a pale cloudy morning laid open the sail's tattered condition. Some of the crew suggested docking at the nearest port; still some waved to the passing boats for help and a few saw impending doom and sat praying with stone beads. Mehraj, the boatswain, a man responsible for the upkeep of sails, sat like a defeated soldier. The crew watched him in distress and mumbled their disapproval. Lines of worry passed across the Captain's wrinkled face and he went about directing his crew to hold on till they reached the warm waters of the gulf. It would make the sailing easier and then there is the God Ahura. *Hail Ahura!* The old man kept chanting in his delirium.

Strangely though, the *Gilgamesh* did not show any sign of either sinking or marooning the crew and sailed on, reaching the Gulf of Amman by the night.

The Captain heaved a sigh of relief. Deep down in his heart, however, he knew that the brig could capsize anytime.

The perilous sailboat carried the crew who waited in fear of the inevitable. Every night the dinner had become a quiet affair and Annarria, the head cook called it the last supper, smiling a weak smile. Have a large helping boy. We might as well finish the stock before the fishes have us with it; he offered a large bowl of vegetable broth and pieces of bread to the tall, red-haired boy, who chomped it hungrily. So, how's our captain, he asked and thanked Annarria saying, if everyday be the last day, we would have the best dinner and a wonderful spread. The head cook admonished him in his fear and told him to keep quiet. Never meddle with the captain, he warned. With one swish of his scimitar he would cut your head off.

The boy's audacity and fearlessness won him an audience with the captain, who, despite sulking, faced up to the youth with the haughtiness of a king. He lighted an ivory smoke-pipe, blew smoke clouds, coughed hoarsely and spat a yellow blob of phlegm and then picked up his scimitar. He pierced the boy's neck with its pointed end threatening him with his red swollen eye.

The boy stood defiantly as a thin stream of blood trickled down staining his tunic.

"So, it seems you have finally decided to lay down your arms which, having lived for countless years is a fair call. A defeated captain is better than a renegade. History will remember you as the one who sunk with his boat and crew," the boy spoke with the conviction of a brave soldier.

"I worry, not for my life but that of what I carry in this doomed sailboat and for which I could lay down my life, but that is none of your concern. Busy as you are of making fun of me and my crew-men. Boy, you don't know under what circumstances we have managed this voyage; neither can I make you believe in what we have been through. Your age is to make merry and of course make toys, as you proclaim to the entire world, so if you wish to fulfill your dream before you die, you better cooperate with us or ..." he pierced the scimitar into the tender skin of the boy who winced in pain.

"What do you imply?" the boy asked.

"That *you* find a way out for us. In our survival is yours. Destiny has brought us on the same boat, literally," the captain said.

"He claims to be a magician and now he owes us a magical show by getting us through this rough patch." Al Fayer, the supervisor of the oarsmen observed.

"I am no magician but a toy-maker certainly. Ah! Tell me who the captain amongst us is?" the boy relaxed knowing his utility in the scheme of things to come.

"True, that I am the leader but it seems we need your expertise which you claim you have to repair the ship," the captain relented and put down his weapon.

"I can mend it for you, make it navigable, but say, what do I get in return?" the boy asked calmly wiping the trickling blood from his neck.

"You have the temerity to make a demand knowing well that you are under the mercy of my scimitar?" the Captain hissed.

"Now, when all is lost, you will throw a last dice and I am that cowry shell which could win you this game, Captain. Let me roll and win this game of *chaupar* for you." the boy eyed the tattered sails and laughed at his predicament. So the endgame cometh, this boat will sink before the next full moon day, he concluded.

"Ah Captain! Tell me who is *Gilgamesh*?" he asked in a quiet sarcasm. "Is it the demi-god who lies under the sea? Call him in to mend this piece of wood."

Destiny plays truant when on one least expects it to, the boy thought, enjoying the freedom from plying the ores as he went about examining the sailboat: the double mast, with a smaller one supporting the mainsail, bulkier and with an army of desolate death fearing crew who rowed with laborious movements; death being a matter of few days. The boy entered the area where two rows of rowlocks whirled with the sound of lazy rowing. Tired men gossiped in between and smoked cheroot whenever Al Fayeer, the tall well-built, mustard-oiled supervisor, stopped beating on the rhythm drum for the rowers to catch a wink.

"Al Fayeer Sir, how goes the speed of rowing?" the boy, carrying his bag, tapped the tall man.

"Thank you for making me a free bird," he smiled in a friendly overture and offered him a few almonds.

"It's a lost cause, sonny. You are lucky as it seems the captain likes your puerile talks so roam about without the burden of laboring," he replied morosely and stared at the rowers.

"I am thinking of ways to get us out of this predicament in which we all find ourselves in and you deride my effort. C'mon, Al Fayeer, I expect a better deal from you. Why don't you row? It would motivate the other rowers to give their best when they see a strong man rowing with them," the boy challenged him.

"Would it?" he asked somewhat relenting at the boy's proposal.

"Why don't you see for yourself?" the boy asked instead.

"Yes I will if you say so. let Russi be he drummer and I will pick up the row." Al Fayeer offered.

"Wait," thundered the boy and faced the rowers.

"Attention my friends…" he shouted at the top of his voice. "Al Fayeer, who till the other day, tortured you if you were slow, is now ready to join you to keep the flicker of hope alive while all of you only talk of the impending doom – of sinking ships and death."

A mumble rose from among the rowers.

"What have you in mind, dear boy?" Nissirii, one of the rowers, asked.

"Isn't it obvious, sir and the rest of you? I want to live. I want to see the bazaars of Melhua, I want to taste the goodies of Harappa, I want to chase the beauties of Chahunjor Kot and I want to reach the ports of Suktangot Dor before our sailboat capsizes," the boy spoke passionately.

A few of the rowers shifted uneasily.

"It is a lost cause, sonny. This ship has the evil eye of Queen Kassandrra of south-west Arianna. She practices black magic to annihilate her enemies and our captain is her sworn enemy. She won't let us live," one of the crew member lamented.

"I see an enemy far more dangerous than your Queen Kassandrra right here in this boat," the boy announced.

"Who is he? Where is he?" a shout echoed.

"Right inside you all – *fear* is its name and *inertia* is its weapon; it spreads like a deathly epidemic and it has no cure," the boy stood on a wooden shaft and addressed the rowers. *It was the first time and the boy was surprised at himself. He talked as if he were a savant, a king, a prophet, a legend.*

"We are battle hardened men. Boy, we have brushed aside death at close quarters, seen our families being erased right in front of our eyes; died a thousand deaths in wars and yet you have the gumption to call us cowards!" Nubli, the strongest of the rowers, rose to his feet and clenched his fists.

"So what has happened now? Why do you give in to destiny now when you all have a chance to re-shape it? Why not rise and fight one last battle before all ends?" the boy implored.

"But we are fighting a lost battle. This ship has been aging and it's just a matter of time before it sinks. No, boy, we can't do much. The Gutien warriors will soon be tailing us to nail us down. This is the end," Nassirii said. "It has been a long long journey, son, we all want a restful sleep and death... is..."

"The journey of life doesn't begin with our free will, neither will it end when we want it to, so we have to trudge along. I agree and I know things cannot get worse. Therefore, my friends, this is the time when we unite and find that *one* thing which will help us survive." The boy didn't let go. "My mother has blessed me to live for hundred and fifty seasons."

"Did she bless you to live for hundred and fifty years?" a chorus arose.

"Indeed, sir, and her blessings have never failed me. They are not a hoax. So if I live you all live. I am the lucky charm in this boat and one should always believe in good luck charms," the boy drove home his point emphatically.

"What could that *one way* be?" Al Fayeer intervened, keen to be a part of the solution to the problem.

"What if we can somehow reach the ports of Suktangot Dor before we sink?" the boy said as he stared at the men.

"We could add that much longevity to our sailboat," Nassirri replied.

"And how is that possible?" Nubli asked.

"By rowing faster and faster and not stopping till we reach the ports of Melhua," the boy answered as he got down from the wooden plank and caught hold of the rope to climb on to the navigating bridge.

"How is that possible... er... to increase our speed?" Nassiri asked hesitatingly.

"That my friends you all have to find out... *together!*" the boy's voice trailed off, leaving the crew befuddled.

The Captain accosted him on the deck. "You have a gift of talking your way out of a piquant situation but are you capable of showing results we are desperately hoping for?" he asked.

"Dear Captain of the Dead Seas, who is older of the two, you or your sailboat?" the boy humoured instead.

A laugh ringed through the boat as the sea-men laughed. The Captain guffawed.

"Take your pick, young man; I am too old to talk of age." he replied and then broke into a chuckle.

The boy laughed freely and with him the seamen and their captain.

"I told you we had a clown in this dying ship," the Captain

sneered and then brandishing his scimitar, asked, "When do we start the repairs, young man?"

"We already have," the boy was calm in his reply.

"Have we? Do you see the sail functioning, Mehraj?" the Captain asked. "Or are the leaks blocked, Dilawari? No progress at all, Ah! The magician has failed, it seems." he stared at the boy.

"And now, boy, before you dive into the sea to escape, let me have the satisfaction of beheading you," the captain raised his scimitar threatening the boy.

"I am just a toy-maker and yet I have made the ship move faster. Haven't you noticed this, Captain of the Seven Seas?" he asked.

"And you all have learnt to laugh at your misery, my friends, *that* is the first step towards *repairing anything… just anything!*" the boy announced in his gayness and climbed on to the bamboo on which hung the tattered mainmast with a felicity of a trapeze artist.

What have I done? Something has gotten into me. The boy was wondering at his new found ability to get things moving. Then he realised that it was the circumstances he faced that had made him look for solutions. He noted in his mind; *Circumstances turn a boy into a man.*

The repair of a tattered sail would indeed be a challenge the boy thought as he swung on the rope tying the only remaining sail and examined the piece of fragile canvas. It was torn at many places around the leech, its gaff was cracked and the halyard needed an extra helping of a strong rope. Little holes could soon become gaping holes.

"We will make a new sail," the boy shouted his resolve.

The Captain watched him impatiently and paced up and down the ship till he could take it no more and shouted at the boy to get down.

"You do your work, Captain," the boy shouted back. "And let

me do mine. Here I am trying to fix your coffin and you go about shouting like a lost shepherd."

"Is there any hope?" the captain asked.

"Is there a reason for drowning hope – the boat in which we all sail through the journey of life?" the boy asked instead and in a swift movement rolled down the mainmast and faced the captain.

Hope is a new word, the boy thought, the use of which makes me feel energetic. It lightens the burden of my problems and it makes my fellow sailors smile. *Hope must be a big word.*

"I will need all the clothing that is available in the ship; I say *all*, every piece of livery, canvas, cotton or jute rugs – just anything which can be sewn and all the ropes. Mehraj will be my assistant," he demanded in his excitement

"And what do you intend to do all that clothing?" the captain asked.

"We start with you, Captain. Your gold brocaded gown, please. You are the captain and you should be the one to set an example by handing it to me," the boy ignored the captain's whining and sat on the floor waiting.

"If I refuse to give my royal robe…" the captain said quietly and yet started unbuttoning his royal robe.

Early in the morning, a warm sun welcomed the ship as it entered the *Ocean Indicus*. The boy sat with his bag and started sewing the mass of clothing into a huge sail. Mehraj knotted it through a huge rope fixing the jib, spreader, batten and leech wherever required. The backstay of the mast was strengthened and the mainmast was tied to the mainsheet.

By the following evening the two had raised the new mast with the help of Al Badari and Burranni. The sailboat had two sails, a mainsail and a smaller supporting one.

The frown on the captain's face had disappeared as he sat playing his banjo with a coral plectrum in his half-pants and smoking his ivory smoke-pipe. The crew could sense a change in mood and they egged on the rowers to ply faster. Some of them even changed places with those who were tired.

A strange bonding developed between the disparate group and the boy moved about telling everyone to be cheerful and jolly and telling them that a sailboat was after all just a toy. But deep inside the boy knew that the leaking ship with the decaying wood panels had a bleak chance to making it to its destination. He climbed down to the stern where Burranni, the person responsible for emptying the leaking water wore a smug look as he went about throwing the water that had collected through the porous wooden planks.

"Will the boat hold?" the boy quizzed.

Burranni ignored the boy and continued with his task.

"Give me the pot and you get some fresh air, or better still; listen to what the Captain is playing."

So saying, the boy snatched the brass utensil from Burranni's tired hands and pushed him up the dangling rope staircase.

"The stars are beautiful, my friend. Go on, read them for us and find the shortest route. Al Fayer says you are the best navigator on board," the boy said.

"Did he say that? I thought he didn't like me and it was because of his advice that I was shunted down to throwing out the leaking water?" Burranni complained.

"No way, Sir! He asked me to send you on to the navigation board. He is with the rowers if you want to wish him a hello," the boy got down to examining the leaks.

The *Indicus Ocean* was calm and the sail was smooth. It made the captain forget his misery and he wondered at the smart solutions the toy-maker applied, turning weary warriors into efficient sea-men. He lamented at the loss of his gold brocaded robe.

"Real gold," he murmured.

"The old man thinketh." the boy strolled in, water dripping from his clothes.

"You did manage to speed up the ship." the captain acknowledged.

"I just ignited in your people the need for a better life and then left them to find their way about. You see, Captain; *crisis brings out the best in us,*" the boy said.

Ah! What has become of me? The boy asked himself. I am speaking a very different language from what I spoke at Nineveh. Perhaps all this travelling and sailing has done me a world of good, he summed up his tryst with wisdom.

"It certainly brought the best out of you, faced as you were with imminent death," the captain brandished his scimitar.

"So I deserve some sort of reward, don't I? This scimitar of yours would do it for me, for the time being. Once we reach Melhua you can gift me pearls," the boy smiled and eyed the rusted weapon longingly.

"My sword! ugh... dear boy of the beasts, this is no ordinary sword," the captain snarled.

"And I don't aspire for ordinary things," the boy was calm.

"It has a history," the captain retorted.

"So do I," the boy faced the old man.

"It belongs to the Ariannic dynasty dear boy. Do you see this symbol of the pepul tree and a horn-headed man? This is the highest authority in the lands of Arianna, and you, a simpleton, aspire for it? Son, you surely aim high," the captain guffawed.

"Oh! I have that very symbol on my amulet which I have right here safely in my bag." The boy examined the weapon carefully.

"So, my dearest old man, I might indeed be the rightful owner of this sword." he gazed at the captain's lone eye.

"Enough of your jokes. Now run along and play with the dancing fishes. You might sight a dolphin," the captain took a deep drag of his smoke-pipe and closed his eyes.

"If you don't believe me then you are welcome to have a look at this," so saying the boy fished out the amulet from his bag and handed it over to the captain.

"My mother said that it would protect me from any misfortune," he spoke wistfully, with teary eyes.

The captain took the amulet and examined it scrupulously, the colour of his face changing as he delved deeper into the mystery of the amulet. He paused and then mumbled. "Did your mother give it to you?"

His body rose in a shiver and a pale shadow rested on his battle-hardened face.

"Yes, old man, now can I please have it back? You don't reward good workers, Captain, learn to encourage people and see how a sense of calm pervades your very being," the boy extended his hand.

The captain closed his eye and suddenly slumped on his seat and murmuring.

"Leila... Leila... my..."

A look of disbelief and dismay rested on his wrinkled face and tears filled his eye.

"Hey Captain...." the boy rushed to his aid.

"Go away, boy... go away...leave me alone..." the captain wailed.

The boy was astonished at the unfolding misery of the captain. He was curious to find out the cause of the pitiable state of his saviour and yet he obeyed the command of the captain and left him alone in his grief.

Black-robed horsemen chased him with swaying swords – hunters on the prowl. The old man rode his white horse with a degree of expertise dodging his assassins, sometimes counter attacking them with his long spear –the sorsa. They chased him to the foothills of the Zagros Mountains. He climbed down the narrow path which led to the streams

and the caves where he could hide. He looked back and counted three horsemen. Thick foliage became his hiding place as he waited for the ambush; then a splurge of blood and cries of the dying. He was a mercenary now, hunting those who hunted him –the Yavannas.

The journey for survival took him to the ruins of Choga Mish which became his home for many a days. Then, disguising as an elderly woman while crossing the city of Susa, he finally hid in the Yafteh caves for many a years – the book Avesta and his faith on Lord Ahura Mazda being his source of living. Time passed till one day a surviving spy of Emperor Kara Indash found him thus saving him from certain death due to starvation and illness. They carried him to an unknown place till he recuperated under the nursing gaze of Ayuriya, a physician from Melhua.

The parcel he carried was safe. But his daughter Leila?

She was supposedly burnt in the fire of the fire temple outside the city of Susa.

The captain woke up in a pool of sweat, his breath uncontrollable and his body shivering in a spasm. With trembling hands he picked up the terracotta mug and sipped the remaining *sura*, wetting his parched lips and smacking his tongue violently. Damn... he swore and searched for the bottle. He pulled a new one from the case and bit the cork with his teeth. He spat it out and placed the bottle on his mouth gulping down half of its content in one breath. The shivering stopped as the captain reclined on the rug and closed his eyes. Destiny sure has a way to strike you when you least expect it to. Now after many a seasons had passed, Leila was back through the boy, he thought.

The oval amulet which the boy carried does prove something but ....

He seems an honest boy, keen to be a toy-maker and no more. At the same time, he does have the capabilities to lead and find solutions and his quick wit was something he inherited from his father. The old seaman slumped on the rug under the influence of liquor and slept, dreaming fearful dreams of deaths and mayhem.

The boy stretched himself and inhaled the sea air; salty and fish smelling. The captain is a good soul, he reflected, but what should I care of. I will concentrate on making toys; not just for the kids to play with, but those which are put alongside the dead. Yes indeed I will make toys to be put in my mother's grave. She would love them – her favourites: a dog, few goats, a peacock, a painted vase, flower beads, an owl, a bird in a nest – they will convey the message that I love her more than ever. The boy was in tears. If only she was alive, then this journey would have been so much fun. Now it was a means to run away from the past.

The Captain walked across his cabin in slow reflective steps; if the boy was his grandson should he be told or should I just let time take its own course? I need his kinship and he needs my affection but he is of an age when parental love shouldn't come in between his love for learning and exploring the microcosm that this universe is. Yes indeed. Knowledge is rational and let him learn it the hard way. Then he would be a man with some merit. Ah! The boy had mentioned shaping his destiny and chasing his dreams, so let him work his way up. The Captain was pleased and decided to let the boy do what he dreamt of doing. If that is his wont, then none can stop him from doing the same. Kalarth is the best artist on the planet at present and he would take the boy under his tutelage. And there will be old man Yatrayavalkya. It has been long since the two of us has played *chaupar*. I will beat him this time around. The Captain smiled as he recalled old memories. That is what it is with the sublime past. It makes the tormented present much bearable. The lazy morning put him into deep slumber.

The sun was strong when he woke up. *Grishm-ritu* is round the corner in these parts of the globe, he thought. We must be nearing the lands of Melhua – the beautiful cities of Chahununjor

Kot and Mohouzeddro will be decked up for the spring festival. But it is at Harappa that the actual fun lies. The Captain smiled and leaned on the ship's railings when at that definitive moment a falcon swished through the air and sunk its claws into his left shoulder. Five pearly drops of blood peeped through his raiment. It would be a matter of time when the Captain bid the mother earth a teary goodbye.

"Hey Captain…wake up!". A few drops of water were sprinkled on his face. Somebody offered him a swig of the *sura*. He felt a sense of dampness descending on him until he passed out again.

On the third day the Captain woke up for a brief while. His bluish body lay in the state of semi-consciousness. His trusted aides encircled him praying that the effect of *ishturr,* the deadly poison which the falcon had transmitted into his blood becomes weak and the Captain survives.

"I am dying," the Captain began to speak incoherently. "Get me the boy."

The boy was called. It had been three days and the boy hadn't eaten a morsel. His eyes were red from crying and he no longer joked or smiled.

"Son," the Captain began, "I see you waste your time grieving on things which aren't in your control. What *is* in your control however, is that you shape your destiny and with it the destiny of people around you. For when you are happy and successful, it becomes your duty to make your fellow-men happy and successful. You want to be a toy-maker and indeed you shall be. Here take this seal to my friend Kalarth who runs an art gurukul and earn his blessings." So saying he handed the boy a terracotta seal.

"Son, in your pursuit of your dreams you should remember three things; read omens, coincidences, hints and clues for they are your good luck charms. Listen to your elders and always pay *dakshina* to the guru you are learning from. Hence for the guidelines I am giving you I want you to do me a favour."

The Captain pulled out a packet from his belongings and handed it to the boy, "Give it to my friend Yatravalkaya and he would know what to do," the Captain coughed a lot of blood and his body shivered spasmodically. With laboured breath he said, "Search for the *Alchemist of the East....*"

The scimitar fell out from his rug and rolled towards the boy's feet. He picked it up. He had read the omen of the weapon finding its true battler.

The boy cried forlornly as the body of the Captain was being kept out in the open on the sailboat's deck for the vultures to feed on. No sooner had the crew sat around the body and closed their eyes praying, thousands of scavengers who wailed with a strange piping sound suddenly appeared and hid the sun. But none of them bit a morsel of the Captain's flesh. It was as if they were lamenting the passing of a blithe and godly soul. The avian creatures formed a huge flower with the backdrop of the blue skies as if saluting the dead Captain. Then in a sudden swoon the birds lifted the carcass of the Captain and carried it away.

The boy was wonderstruck by what the Captain had said. His mother had often told him about omens, charms, instructions, signs and the need to follow the learned men but he had ignored her, even making fun of her for her insistence that he grows into a wise man. Now that she was no more he resolved that he would do what she had desired him to do. He stopped grieving and called Mehraj, the trusted aide of the Captain and asked him what the recent events held for his future.

To begin with he wondered what the packet that he was supposed to take care of contained. "What is this all about?" he waved the goatskin parcel.

"The rules to be followed by a *Mazdayasna*..." Mehraj replied.

The boy was inquisitive now. He loved to solve the puzzles and then he realised that the best way to forget one's grief was to keep oneself busy with one mystery or the other.

"The *Mazdayasna*... the God worshipper." Mehraj clarified.

"*Mazdayasna*! Why my mother mentioned it to me once," the boy was further intrigued. He knew that something momentous was about to unfold.

"She worshipped Lord Ahura .." The boy mumbled.

"*Ahu* means the *living* and *Ra* means *to give*. Hence Ahura means the life giver," Mehraj replied solemnly.

"So this packet contains the secrets of Ahura?" the boy asked.

"Son, do what has been told by the Captain. I have already told you enough. You should search for Yatravalkavya and hand him the packet," Mehraj replied.

"Who is Yatravalkavya?" the boy asked.

"The chief advisor of the Sapta Sindhu Confederacy and it is he who has been destined to tell you the tale of the Captain and his valour. I have to carry out the last wishes of the Captain and he had asked me to lead you to Guru Kalarth. Look far away into the horizon, son. We can see the lights of the port city of Suktogan Dor. It is through the application of your common sense and the valour of the Captain that we have been able to safely reach the land of seven rivers." Mehraj closed his eyes and mumbled a prayer.

"And who is the *Alchemist of the East*?" the boy asked impatiently.

"You are impetuous, my son. The Lord has ordained that I do what I have been asked to do. It is up to you to find who the alchemist is," so saying Mehraj left the boy.

On seeing the high security walls of the town of Sutkogan Dor, the boy gave a loud cry of cheer and thanked Lord Ahura. The blue waters of the Dasht River mingling with the muddy waters of the Gojo Kaur stream enlivened his mood and he whistled his approval. New places make old grief tolerable, he noted.

The crew danced in gay abundance celebrating the success of their voyage, shouting in delight and hugging each other with tears of joys rolling down from their tired eyes.

The sailboat sailed on the river Dasht searching for a dock. Al Fayer couldn't find a docking place as the dockyard overflowed with ships those from Mesopotamia, Egypt, Yemen, Syria and Ethiopia. It was a busy trade route and some ships from Lothal could be seen leaving the port for their journey westward.

The boy suggested that for a while they could anchor at the mouth of smaller stream of Gojo Kaur. The water was clean and we all need a proper washing, otherwise we would be termed as sick and quarantined for many a nights, he reasoned.

He was happy to reach the ports and heaved a sigh of relief. He moved about thanking the rowers and wishing them luck for a better future. Remember, future is always a thousandfold better than the past and a hundredfold better than the present; he proclaimed much to the delight of the ragged and tired bunch of mariners.

The evening had set in and the lights of the town of Sutkogan Dor were visible, shining invitingly at the tired crew but Mehraj had ordered them not to move about the town until immigration conditions were met and the relevant seals exchanged. There are strict rules in the Sapta-Sindhu, he had warned and left hurriedly for his meeting with the officials of the port city.

The boy roamed the banks of the river making sand castles as the sun bid adieu for the day. Tomorrow will be a new day, nay a new life, he concluded and picked up the shells from the sands, cleaning some and throwing away the ones he disliked. He wondered about how his life had changed since last few weeks. He thought of the Captain and his followers. They are the family I had and now even they would all be gone to pursue their respective dreams. So have I, yes indeed the art gurukul is my calling and then perhaps a meeting with Yatravalkavya. The boy slept and dreamt of his mother holding his hands telling him that parents never die and they are always nearby to help their children. She sang him lullabies and he slept the sweetest sleep he had slept for a long time.

The morning was full of fun as a boat from Kalibangan had docked on the port, carrying a bunch of colourfully attired singers from the Thar dessert who sang songs of love and ballads of longing. The cook Annaria treated the crew to a sumptuous breakfast of milk and millet cakes and then Mehraj addressed them.

"Friends, I have done the necessary documentation for your immigration, and Meer will distribute the relevant seals. I bid you good bye as I will be moving on to Harappa for a meeting with Yatrayavalkaya. You all are free to pursue your passions but leave your forwarding address to Meer in case I need your services. The boy here has done wonderful work for us, so on behalf of all of you I extend him a heartfelt thanks and I will get him admitted to the art gurukul of Guru Kalarth according to the last wishes of the Captain where he can pursue his dream of becoming a toy-maker."

The seamen clapped, cheered and hugged each other with tears in their eyes and a promise to meet in the near future. Meer had decided to stay at the port city and open up an adventure unit as he loved to travel, Al Fayeer sought to travel further east and train the army of Chahunjor Kot, for they were great fighters and who knows there might be a war soon, he reasoned. Al Badari told everyone that he wanted to write about the Captain's adventures and hence would settle at a quiet hill station near Ammari in the Kirthar Mountains.

The boy tailed Mehraj carrying the packet with him. He had made a scabbard and placed the old rusted sword in it and walked with haughty steps.

Russi, Nassirri, Burrani and Nubli had decided to move east

towards the rich plains of the River Sindhu where large farms of rice and wheat were aplenty and in dire need of farm hands. Annaria had found a café where he could experiment with his culinary skills. Dilawari was keen to join a ship which was bound for Lothal. The boy wondered at the unfolding of many dreams and concluded that there are as many dreams as there are humans. It made him happy that he was in some way responsible of keeping their dreams alive. And when dreams are alive, humanity is in tune with the universal consciousnesses, his mother had told him .

"*I am a dream merchant*", the boy shouted in delight.

Soon the two were on their way, riding a bullock cart driven by a young tribal boy. "Are you happy now that you will soon be pursuing your dream?" Mehraj asked.

"Yes and er… no… for the death of the Captain fills my heart with remorse as well as a sense of vague responsibility. I wonder what the contents of this packet foretell," the boy narrated his apprehensions.

"This packet contains all the treasures of the world with words written in gold. However, you will have to work hard so that they reveal their true meaning to you. They are not mere words. They are treasure in the form of letters. And since the words are invaluable a lot of people would want them for their narrow personal gains. Who knows what you have to encounter to keep the packet safe? If you lose it then it would pain the soul of the Captain."

"Why can't I know what is in this goatskin wrapper, *now*?" the boy was exasperated.

"There is always a right time for everything one does or is destined to do. You have to learn the elementals of fulfilling your dreams. Thinking doesn't take anyone anywhere. Action does. A man has to work and prosper, not rest and rust. Until you faced death you had been rusting in the city of Nineveh. Once you came out of your comfort zone, which itself was brought about by the untimely demise of your parents, you worked hard to survive and now you know how to sail, repair a boat and motivate people. Your hard work won the heart of even the battle hardened Captain who chose you to carry on his legacy. He wanted to tell me something a night before he died but stopped short of emptying his soul. He wanted you to learn the art of mastering one's fate by hard and honest work," Mehraj sermonised.

The boy was silent for most of the remaining journey as it opened his mind to the the green earth and blue waters and varied flora and fauna. The earth throbbed with keen energy and sublime secrets. The boy wanted to know all about mother earth.

"Nature is all we need to have to be able to live, love and learn," he mumbled joyfully.

On the third day of steady riding they reached the village of Valerezi, a pretty village situated on the rain shadow region of the Kaimer hills. Keer, a crystal clear blue water stream flowing besides it added to its charm and mystique. Its climate remained predominantly dry with many a sunny days and a temperature and air most suitable for terracotta art and sculpting. A thick deciduous forest hid the small hamlet of assorted hay huts with lovely gardens, sparkling fountains and an exhibition of terracotta art. This was Guru Kalarth's Art Gurukul.

Mehraj seemed to be a well known man as the procter of the college; a youngish man called Yathavat came to greet him and quickly arranged for their boarding and lodging.

In the morning they were led to the guru's hut.

Kalarath was a stout man with a bearded face, keen eyes and flowing white hair. The boy entered with tentative steps as strange fears and bouts of nervousness attacked him.. He was just a step away from accomplishing what he had always dreamt of. It was at this moment he realised that the last step was always the hardest.

He stood in sombre attendance, his head bowed in awe and admiration of the great guru. In all his nervous admiration the boy fell at the master's feet.

"My blessings to you, my son. My boundless blessings to the one who believes in his dreams..." the guru mumbled as he patted the red hair of the boy.

"Hand him the seal of the Captain," Mehraj directed the boy.

The boy did as told. Guru Kalarth read the Captain's message with reverence and fondness of friendly remembrances. His eyes were teary for a while.

"Hmm...so you want to learn terracotta art?" the guru asked. "The Captain was my friend and I grieve his passing away but his reference is not the final word when it comes to getting admitted into our gurukul. Merit is. Are you ready to undergo a small test?" he asked.

"Yes... y-e-s...Gurudev.I am..." the boy stammered.

"Do you know anything about the Nall style of painting?"

The boy thought for a while and then said 'No... Gurujee... I am... sorry.

"Have you heard of the Ammri style of terracotta art?" the guru asked again.

The boy shook his head and for many a question he was asked he kept shaking his head, for he didn't know the answers to any of them.

He was given soft clay and asked to make a toy bird. He did but Kalarth brushed aside the boy's effort as the fancy of a child. A piece of wood was given to the boy and he was asked to chisel a bull. Again the guru refused to acknowledge the talent of the boy.

A dismayed boy asked for a piece of chalk and made drawing on the stone slab but the guru shooed the boy away asking him to forget his dream of being an artist.

"I am afraid your dream is in the realm of poor imagination and false pretence. You have lied to yourself about your dreams without working for them. Worse, you have failed to cultivate feelings and imagination which will help you to make the most delicate and fine structures in your mind. You are not the poet who can understand the Soul of the Universe and paint it as if it were right in front of his eyes." the guru prepared to leave.

The boy couldn't hide his disappointment. Nobody had spoken to him thus. He regretted that he met the guru so late in his life. He fell on Kalarth's feet. "Please Gurujee, I will do anything, even menial work but please let me just stay here under your tutelage. I can cook for you, sweep the floor and bring in the water from the stream but please don't leave me when I need you the most," the boy wailed.

Kalarth bend down and hugged the boy. "You had come with your cup filled to the brim with your set of preconceived notions and boasting of trivial achievements. Now you are the empty vessel which can carry my teachings and make full use of them for yourself and use them to serve humanity. Yes indeed you will be my pupil. But you will have to work for me as I don't think you can afford to pay up my fees – the *dakshina*."

"I will, Gurujee...I will carry out your directions as if they were the words of my mother." Tears rolled down the boy's eyes like streams of happiness.

Soon it was time for Mehraj to leave. "I will meet you soon, he said. Destiny had brought us close and your getting into the famed gurukul of art is destiny too. Now you are on your own with a guru to guide you. Bake yourself, son, in the fire of learning and gather information and instruction from everywhere. It is when you are alone with your dreams that God enters your life and shows you the path."

With these parting words of Mehraj bid the boy goodbye as he rode a bullock cart and disappeared in the dusty cloud, far into the horizon, like a blithe waif.

The boy remained grumpy for days. The new session was still a few days away and the boy worked hard to impress his guru, carrying out the teacher's orders like the words of the lord. In the evenings he would sit by the stream and recall what his mother had tried to teach him when he was a kid. He had ignored her then. She had said *"Think for yourself but never through others.'"*

"Yes mother, I will and I will listen to omens and to my heart and I will serve my guru. I will make toys to be put in a pyramid I will make for you" the boy shouted.

It was then that the last words of the Captain came back to haunt him.

Look for the Alchemist of the East....

The boy succumbed to the charms of the mystery hanging like a noose around his neck. Surprisingly it didn't suffocate him; on the contrary it liberated him from futile living. Yes, a purpose, a search is important for one to lead a successful life. In him had grown a feeling of imminent greatness, a queer unrest which cajoled him to seek perfection in whatever he did.

He was not the boy who had left the banks of River Tigris anymore. *He had changed.* He had a purpose to achieve his dreams.

One day as he sat with his group of friends that he had made in the gurukul, a colourful bull chariot entered the gurukul compound and was immediately surrounded by a bevy of giggling girls. A diminutive girl with long black hair and a mystical aura floating around her got down from the chariot and hugged the complaining girls. A commotion ensued as she tried to placate them with promises and assurances of a jolly time ahead. She then led a procession of sorts to her hostel room on the far right corner of the art gurukul.

The crowd cheered and hailed her the new messiah of the gurukul as she said she had brought silken dresses for everyone and that the next full moon day there would be a grand picnic organised by her on the banks of the stream. "Hail...Yatrayamini... hail... Yatrayamini. She is our heroine and our saviour. The love of our life," the girls shouted in unbound joy.

On way, the procession ran into the boy and his gang of friends; *Fakhira* they had named it thus.

A brouhaha rose as the boys and the girls fought for a passage across the narrow courtyard.

"Excuse us, will you?" the girl shouted. "How has this group of *junglees* entered the famed gurukul of arts?" she asked angrily.

"It is *he*." One of her friends whispered, pointing eagerly towards the boy.

"Yatrayamini let us go; *he* is not worth talking to," the other friend pulled at her warp.

"I am not of afraid of anyone lest of all a newcomer," Yatrayamini stood her ground and eyed the boys with contemptuous glee.

"C'mon boys, let go of the poor girls. They need time to gossip about clothes and gorge upon food," the boy spoke with a quiet sarcasm.

"Are you making fun of us?" Yatrayamini faced the tall boy.

"C'mon girl, preserve your energy to create. We aren't the monkey fighters, moreover who wants to deal with a petite girl like you?" the boy smiled calmly. "Little red riding riddle diddle do diddle do" he sang.

"Little red riding riddle diddle do diddle do…" the boys chorused, repeating the boy's humming.

"Control your tongues, you rogues! Don't you have manners of the ones befitting the students of this famed gurukul? Don't you know how to talk to the girls and not tease them like wild roadies? Do you know who I am?" she was furious.

"Don't dare me, or else." It was the boy's turn to get angry and threaten her.

"Or else, or else… what? Will you hit me?" Yatrayamini was indeed very angry.

"I won't hit you but I can make a clay idol of you for little children to play with and laugh over it or even better just morph it into a macabre face so that it could to be put on the entrance of every house in Harappa to ward off an evil eye," the boy laughed, enjoying his rendezvous with a beautiful, mysterious and fiery girl.

"So you are some sort of a toy-maker?" she asked cautiously.

"Indeed I am and one day I will be known for this art. I have come all the way from Mesopotamia to learn it from Gurudev Kalarth," he spoke passionately.

"Oh! So you are the one. Did you know the Captain?" she asked, somewhat calmed now.

"Yes I did, but I couldn't save him," the boy lamented.

"You did your best," she laid a comforting hand on his shoulders. "I am sorry…"

A sudden calmness engulfed the boy like the pleasant air or the warm sun on a cold day. He made way for her and asked for her forgiveness.

"It is alright, we are young and we can always have some fun," she smiled beatifically.

"Let us go girls. He is a guest in our lands and hence deserves our respect," she called out to her companions.

"Thanks for a little consideration,"the boy called out and waved his long hands.

"Who cares?" Yatrayamini whispered and picked up her baggage and moved towards her room.

Strange girl, thought he; hers is some tantrum, more than her tiny structure could hold on to. Her hair, I haven't seen such long and flowing tresses for a while. She walks with an assured gait, quite unlike the girls of Mesopotamia who are followers of their warrior husbands. No wonder the Sapta-Sindhu boosts of beauty with brains.

Strange boy, thought she, too tall for my liking. Despite his penchant for creating nuisance he has an air of an easy going guy. He has the grit and determination of the one who has seen it all, having risen from the ranks, struggled on roads and denied of basic care; but he still dreams. Only that he is too self assured, bordering on arrogance.

The Art Gurukul

"Art is a culmination of all that one stands for," Guru Kalarth addressed the assembly of his chosen students. "We are here to refine what you already have. Yes, we will be giving shape to a lump of mud or a piece of wood. Giving it meaning and hence life. True, we will dig for the softest earth and shape our dreams, sculpting it into various forms but what we actually do is to give our own self a vision. Yes, dear students, we dream and we actualise those which are closest to our hearts. The ones for which we sacrifice all that we have. And I assure you that once you are through with the process, you will emerge as persons who you will be proud of." Guru Kalarth paused and then began again. "This is the beginning of a new session and I welcome all those who have joined us and assure them of quality education. In return they should promise us that they will never degenerate or demean whatever they learn. All art is the finest form of *tapasaya* – practice. What are we but the sum total of our habits and lifestyle? Vow to develop a liking for music, literature and arts, for without them a person is like a tailless animal, running in circles to catch the non-existent." So saying the guru took his anointed seat.

The assembly broke thereafter and the students headed towards the open lawns for refreshments.

"I hear the Captain and his band of followers found you in the desert near the banks of Tigris where the vultures where keen to feed on you," Yatrayamini accosted the boy with a pot of lemon juice in her hand.

"Indeed he did and he gave me a direction in life, the one which was mired deep into the ruins of my hopes. Now I find myself among people like you in this famed gurukul," he replied solemnly as he nibbled on a piece of barley cake.

"You talk a lot of wise things. Where have you learnt all this?" she asked inquisitively as she sipped her drink, rolling the sweet sour liquid in her mouth.

"My mother was my first tutor and then the hard life I have lived has taught me to value learning and I have unflinching faith in the power of wisdom," the boy said, but he knew that he was unsure about the words he had spoken and he didn't believe in what he had said. *He was trying to impress the girl.* It made the boy uneasy, even guilty of his boastfulness.

"Good for you and then you will make toys which look like Guru Kalarth," she made a serious face and laughed. "Have fun, boy, and you will live younger and longer."

"I am weighed by the questions I face," he said suddenly as if she was the one who could solve most of his queries.

"Time answers most of our questions. Have patience," she left him in a spur of a moment and moved to a tree shade near the temple.

The boy followed hypnotised by her aura, her mystic and her ethereal beauty. For him she belonged to some other universe and had come on visitation to this planet, and *she talks sense* he mused.

"How do you know there is many a universe?' she asked surprising him by following him in her thoughts.

"I sort of guessed. If one wants to know more about you, how does one go about it?' he smiled eagerly.

"Well, you are right in deciphering the universe. The collection of many a universe is called *Brahamand* – the single spiritual entity which belongs to each one of us who resides in this planet," she replied earnestly.

"Have some fun, girlie, you will live longer and younger,' he poked her.

She seemed miffed and then asked him why he had come at a time when the entire Sapta Sindhu confederacy was in upheaval of the most alarming nature.

"Dear girl, I come from a region which is perpetually in strife and yet we are the cradle of modern civilisation. Some creations are preceded by disturbances and destruction," he spoke morosely.

"You are sounding like a cynic," she noticed his despondency. "Your baby face, freckled and pimpled, doesn't owe up your philosophising on such matters," she teased him.

"You are right, a pang of homesickness, I suppose. But yes, why worry, we are creators and hence should have control over our senses and all else," he tried to be cheerful. "You are a petite girl and you talk of millions of universes as if you visit them for a daily walk," he prodded her.

"You wear a lovely amulet," she changed the subject.

"I will make one for you once I complete my basic course," he blushed.

So the two bantered along till the bell for the dinner was sounded and the motley group of students rushed to the dining hall.

The autumn semester was under way and the students got busy with their practical sessions and the preparations for the ensuing winter exams. The boy was to examine the 'Impact of Amri art on the Sapta-Sindhu Terracotta', and he diligently researched, collected items, made terracotta models and even travelled to nearby art villages and met people to collect data for his thesis.

Yatrayamini, on her part was busy with learning the fine art of textile designing and colour mixology. Her patterns on cotton were already the talk of the art world and the bazaars of Asia Minor were keen to sign her as their official designer. It surprised her too, to find a depth and meaning that had crept in her art effort. Maybe the lotus posture she practiced had helped her refine herself, she thought.

In the art gurukul, of particular interest were a few toys made by young students. They were not beautiful, nay one would find them to be ugly, and yet they had a charm of their own. The kids loved these toys and their popularity reached across the oceans to Mesopotamia, Yemen, Syria and the land of Greeks. Priests were common models to be made into terracotta statues; they were always portrayed in some yog asana or other. Alabaster sculptures were also popular among the students and still some of them preferred the stone chiseling of nature symbols and carving of demi-gods on rocks.

Then one day, the boy sculptured a statue of Proto-Shiva, the three headed god. Guru Kalarth explained that it is said that Lord Shiva had three mothers and hence he is depicted with three heads. It impressed Yatrayamini to no end and she begged the boy to give it to her.

"I want that statue. Oh how beautiful the lord looks chiseled as he is on a blue stone!" she exclaimed.

"Hmm... we will see," the boy replied laconically.

"I am ready to pay for it," Yatrayamini offered.

"Didn't you pay heed to what the Gurujee had said?" he replied.

"I want this statue," she was adamant.

"You are a pest of a girl," he sounded miffed.

"Am I?" she asked innocently.

"And no amount of your pretentious innocence will win me over," he declared.

"Make a sugar toy for her," one of the friends of the boy joked as he joined the duo.

"You could be Sushyo's friend, but keep off this transaction between us," Yatrayamini warned the young boy.

"I have told you I won't give it to you," the boy spoke categorically.

"I beg you," she was in tears.

"No..."

Yatrayamini wiped her teary eyes and walked back to her room.

"Now she will make those horrible ornaments that girls wear," the boy's friend laughed. "Good for her, she thinks that she can lord over us, just as her father lords over the Sapta Sindhu."

"Uh hmm... who is her father?" the boy asked.

"Yatravalkavya."

On the next full moon gathering, Yatrayamini found a parcel and a bunch of white roses lying carelessly on her table.

She pulled out the blue stone statue of Shiva and closed her eyes in piety. Her face flushed with radiance and her heart beat to the tune of faith music.

On the coming weekend a visit was organised to the village of Sehwan, where stayed an old man, an expert in the art of making seals. Valuable tips came the way of the students and the boy was amazed by the role of seals in all walks of life of the residents of Sapta Sindhu. The use of these seals were catching up in the world and soon the entire world would be using them in place of barter, he forethought.

The other study tour was to the village of Sikhari.

One day they were told about gold finery and pearl polishing.

The syllabus covered the Amri, Kulli, Mehi and Greeko-Roman arts, which inspired the boy to sculpt a statue of Helen of Troy.

Guru Kalarth was awestruck by the boy's effort and he showed it to the entire school. Sushyo was the new hero of the school and he proudly showed the statue around.

Six months had passed thus and the boy forgot all about the packet and what the Captain had asked him to find out –*The Alchemist of the East...*

Then one day, when the current semester was about to end an attempt was made to steal the packet which had been kept under Kalarth's safe custody. Two Emgroo spies, tall, dark and well armed with stone weapons had stealthily entered the guru's hut and tried to open the iron chest in which the packet had been stowed. Of course they couldn't, for Guru Kalarth was an expert in designing impregnable chests and tough to crack locks. The watchman spotted the two black men and immediately chased them away.

Kalarth knew the time had come for the boy to move on and meet Yatravalkavya.

"Son, do you know what your name means?" he asked the boy.

"Sushyo...hmm... I don't know, Gurujee, my mother called me Sushyo with motherly affection," the boy replied.

"Have you heard of Sushyont and his role in the evolution of humanity?" the guru asked.

"No…" the boy replied but was inquisitive knowing that even names could shape one's destiny.

"Sushyont is the mythical hero in the holy book *Avesta* who rises to crush all evil," the guru informed him. "Now as you have learnt about arts it is time you move on to learn other things. Sushyont, apart from one's dreams, one should follow one's duty, too. It is duty which separates men from boys and now you are a man."

Ah! Too much to learn, the boy sighed. Dream, duty, upliftment of humanity, crushing of evil! I am a toy-maker and no more, the boy thought.

"As you command Gurujee, I was a vagrant but your care and guidance has made me what I am today," the boy spoke concealing what lay in his heart.

"Then follow Yatrayamini. She knows what is to be done and remember, son, be wise enough to take nobody for a fool. You have my blessings," the great guru knew that the boy's calling was someplace else.

The City of Harappa

Next morning Sushyo and Yatrayamini set out for the city of Harappa, which was the capital of the Sapta Sindhu confederacy.

They rode the bullock cart on the Mehergarh highway and took a detour towards a ten-mile bricked pathway along the banks of the the river Parushini which lead to the city of Harappa. At the entrance, there was a huge gate made of wooden logs of sal trees and a column of baked bricks held these wooden poles and the huge doors. A high wall encircled the city, providing the first line of defence to its inhabitants. The city gates were manned by the town *rakshaks*; the guards who are responsible for the basic safety of its residents. The streets were well laid and crossed each other at right angles ensuring a well laid out civic plan built on sound scientific principles. A carefully crafted drainage system was maintained to manage the flow of the water during the rainy season and to avoid outflow of water. Round mud bins were placed at key places to collect household waste. A bullock cart stood in attendance to ferry the waste to the waste disposal plant on the outskirts of the city once the mud bins had been filled to the brim.

It was at the centre of the town, known as the Citadel, where important public buildings were located; a fire temple to worship fire deity Agni, an old temple of Lord Pashupati and other deities: Varuna, Indra, Yakshajanas and the Unicorn. A huge granary for storing grains, an assembly hall for meeting of city officials and a great bath for community bathing, formed the other important public utilities of the city.

"Wow!" he boy cried in amazement as he saw the city and immediately fell in love with it. All he wanted to do was to settle down and open up a toy shop, he told Yatrayamini who eyed him with contempt. Things are not what they seem, she announced. Soon we will be faced with many a problem. You will come to know of them in due course of time, she warned him. He ignored her and eyed the bazaars with a hungry glee.

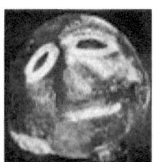

Yatravalkaya emerged from the pool and dabbed his wet body with a cotton towel. He bid goodbye to his fellow bathers and dressed up in the dressing room, wearing his white silken robe and tying his saffron cotton waistband. He brushed his long hair with a coral comb, arranged his flowing beard and moved out into the streets, walking with swagger and swinging his staff every now and then. It was a crowded evening during the *Grisham-ritu* with people thronging the bazaars for the summer fare of ice dollies and cool lime and coconut water.

The duo accosted him in his saunter. Yatrayamini got down from the bullock cart and rushed towards her father.

"My daughter!" Yatravalkya hugged her. "You should have informed me about your holidays, I could have sent my personal charioteer to fetch you. Who is this strapping young man?" he glared at the boy.

"He is Sushyont," she informed her father.

Yatravalkya stood his ground for a long time lost in his thoughts and then hugged the boy and held his hands.

"The Captain and I were friends; he has sent a packet for me."

"Yes, Sir, he has and has he left me with a lot of questions," the boy replied diligently.

"It is destiny which takes you to people who have the answers to your questions," Yatravalkya mumbled.

The trio walked through the bazaars with heavy steps, the memories of Captain seldom leaving them.

In the evening, under a soft yellow light of a lamp, Yatravalkya told Sushyont all about his lineage and the legacy he was about to inherit.

"Son it was the time when the dark ages had set in in the Greek civilisation and the ruling tribe, the Myneansians, suffered at the hands of the Sea People, also known as the Dorians, who came from around the Black Sea, the Aegean area and the Anatolian region. They had knowledge of iron smelting which they had learnt from the Cyprrusians and the Levant. So the edged weapon became the cause of the end of the great Greek civilisation. New states emerged; Sparta, Thebes, Athens, being the most powerful. The invaders also established their own leagues know by various names like; Peleset, Tijekar, Shakalash, Deriyen and Weshesh and simultaneously got rid of the old and weak population of the Greek cities. The strong men and the beautiful girls were forced into slavery. Some of them accepted the new rulers as their masters and continued to support the invaders by doing menial work; they were known as Helots-the lesser ones and were given an inferior status in the city states that emerged in the Greek states. Some though, refused to accept the suzerainty of the attackers and ran away from Greece of yore.

However, they were chased by their attackers and brutally put to horrible deaths. Only a few were able to make it to their freedom. These survivors formed the Greek diaspora, setting down in the islands of Italy, the Mediterranean region and going as far as Libya and Africa," Yatra paused to sip some water.

"One family, headed by a proud old man headed to the land of Arianna, keen to settle down in the Mashkid and Ladiz area in Sistan. The Medes emperor welcomed them and assigned them the vast deserts of Dasht-e-Kavir. The old man was the great grandfather of Kassandrra, the present queen of the Greek Empire in south-west of Arianna; which is bound by the Zagros Mountains from the west and by Dasht-e-Kavir, in the east. Her capital is the ancient city of Susa and under her alliance are the thirteen Medes States of Sistnava region and a few Gutien tribes of Asia Minor," Yatravalkya sighed.

"Aenesidemos, Kassandrra's grandfather, was the old man who worked hard at greening the deserts of Dasht-e-Kavir. His knowledge of agriculture and the cropping patterns, the fertility of soils, the identity of weeds, digging of ground for water and rain water harvesting along with a will to work hard and against all odds, turned the deserts of Dasht-e-Kavir into an oasis of prosperity. His persistence won him the patronage of the Median rulers and he was allowed to set up a Greek colony in the fertile lands of the Mashkid region. To begin with, the colony had five families," Yatra paused for a while and began again.

"The old man had two sons Adeimanthos and Aetes, both from the Greek woman Helen, whom he had bought from the bazaars of Babylon. Both married the local Median tribe girls. Adeimanthos had three daughters: Leto, Adonia, Aella. Aetes had three sons: Carpus, Briarus and Castor. Castor, the youngest and the most ambitious of the lot, married the step sister of Queen Sheeba while on a visit to Syria for trade, winning her over with his valour and disarming smile. The queen gave him expensive gifts, a band of Emgroo slaves, gold coins and many horses and elephants and hundreds of Bantu slaves to look after the animals as part of the dowry. This made him the powerful leader of the group and the two brothers, though older to him, had no choice but to follow him. Castor followed an expansionist policy and built up an army of his own. Knowing his plan for a greater Greece, the Greek royalty of Troy and the rich merchants of Sicily started funding his attacks to the nearby tribal settlements. Soon Castor was a feared name among the Meden traders who were forced to pay him large sums of money in return for a safe passage through the Gulf of Amman. The Meden emperor Kara Indash came to know of his grand designs and led a huge army against him. Castor had a lovely wife and a lovelier daughter, whom he named Kassandrra. Her birth was followed by the birth of her seven brothers," Yatravalkya paused again.

"The armies of Kara Indash ravaged the Greek colony and Kassandrra was taken as a concubine-in-waiting by the emperor. She served his queens in his harem, learning the fine art of enticing men from them. Her seven brothers: Ghandymedes, Eleusis, Hippias, Thon, Zeuxis, Eos and Xanthus, worked in the emperor's army, tending to the horses and maintaining the armory. Zeuxis was a year younger to Kassandrra and considered himself as the eldest of the Greek clan," Yatravalkya closed his eyes and asked for a pot of milk. He drank a few sips and began again.

"Kassandrra grew into a beautiful woman with large green eyes, dark hair and lavender skin. She had a way with men and soon she had many suitor in the court of the emperor, who himself fell for her charms. He married the daughter of the Captain, Leila, instead."

"So the Captain was the general in the courts of Emperor of Arianna?" the boy interrupted.

"Indeed." Yatra admonished the boy.

" Zeuxis was angry at his sister being deprived of her rightful place besides the emperor, who had promised to make her a queen."

Yatravalkya was seemingly tired and paused repeatedly. He seemed to be weighed down by the rendition of a painful history. He began again.

"It was Kassandrra herself who took the lead in organising fellow Greeks in Arianna and broke through the ranks of the Meden tribe using her charms. The Gutien tribe, who were at loggerheads with Kara Indash, sided with her," he sipped the milk and continued.

"When Leila was impregnated, the emperor lost interest in Kassandrra and sent her to the mountain retreat of Zagros. It was here that she came in contact with Sutean tribes who practiced black magic. Before Leila could give birth to her child, the emperor was found dead one day, drowned in his bath tub, his body contorted beyond recognition. Three of Kassandrra's brothers hounded Leila and the trusted aide of the emperor. Leila was soon spotted at a fire temple outside the city of Susa and an unexplained fire killed her with her unborn baby. Since Emperor Kara Indash had died without an heir, Kassandrra was proclaimed the Queen of South-West Arianna and her brothers became the members of her cabinet. Just one glitch remained; the holy book *Avesta* was not to be found anywhere in the palace. The Captain had run away with the holy book which legitimised the rulers of Arianna and made them the direct descendants of the gods. He was never found and was supposed to be dead and the old testament of *Avesta* was supposed to have been destroyed by him. The *Avesta* was to be re-written under the diktats of the queen. The parcel you brought to me is the book *Avesta*. The queen wants it badly." Yatra sighed for he knew that the events that were about to unfold were the very same which he had tried to avoid all through his life.

"And who killed the Captain?" the boy asked.

"The falcon belonged to Prince Zeuxis," the old man said.

The Haunting Past

The boy spent a sleepless night. He couldn't fathom the old man's tale. But the degree of evilness that existed in the world surprised him and it pained him to know that greed could make fellow humans kill others. I was lost in the wonderful and mystical world of toys and now all of a sudden I have to face all this deceit, cunningness and the fear of death, the boy mumbled to himself. Who was Kara Indash? And Queen Leila? How did he have the amulet which had the royal insignia on it?

It was the provoking chirping of the birds which woke him up. Yatrayamini was standing near his bed with a pot full of herbal tea. "Have this broth and clear your mind of whatever dirt my father had filled it with last night," she beamed with a rare intensity.

The boy took a few sips and smiled meaningfully.

"What do you mix in this, a magic potion or a love..." he found himself unabashed. It surprised him and he was ashamed of what he had said to his hostess.

"You needn't be sorry for what you feel and say," she said. "To be honest with one's emotions is a thousand times better than to be silent about what one doesn't feel. Feelings make us all human," she sat beside him.

"I have many a questions pestering my mind. When my mother died I wanted to kill myself but a strange force kept me alive and now when I have been trained to be a toy maker, I feel my calling isn't what I had thought it to be. A vulgar unease pervades my being. And there is a lingering fear of immense pain and foreboding," the boy was morose as he spoke.

"One can never know what one can be or what one has to do," she comforted him with her mystical smile.

He sipped the broth and made a macabre face. "Yuck…" he shouted. "What have you made me drink?"

"Something to keep you off me," she claimed humorously.

"You are a witch of the first degree," he laughed. "That is what you are, weaving magic around me and forcing me to live every moment of my life and teaching me to accept change as the sole mantra of life."

"Isn't it the real mantra of life?" she asked. "Now get ready we have to go and meet Rishi Angiras. He is the learned one and he has all the answers to all the questions about this world and the rest of them."

Soon they were on way to meet the rishi who was working on the sixth *mandala* (book) of the *Rig Veda*. He headed the assembly of the learned who were busy with researching and compiling the first book of knowledge which humanity would ever know.

"We cannot ignore the contribution of the *Avesta* to the writings of the Rig Veda," Yatravalkaya informed them.

"Indeed, Gurudev. If the Captain sacrificed his life for the book it must contain the Soul of the Universe," the boy mumbled.

The father-daughter duo watched the boy closely. Then Yatravalkya asked. "Who told you about the Soul of the Universe?"

"My mother. She had mentioned it to me once but I had

forgotten all about it until now," the boy replied wondering as to how he remembered the words he had ignored. *They have a completely different meaning now...*

Damn... what is it that is changing? I or the world around me? He questioned.

"She was a great soul," the old man replied.

"You knew her?" the boy exclaimed.

"Yes I did," Yatravalkya replied. "But let us rush to the rishi's ashram. We have to be there before sunset."

The bullock cart raced on the gravelled path.

Rishi Angiras was talking with a flowing white beard. His long hair was knotted in neat ropes and rounded off in a bun. Around him hung an aura which pulled the three of them into its fold. He was sitting in the lotus posture and welcomed them with an innocent smile.

"Ah Yatra! It seems you have brought your children on a stroll to my ashram. Come... come my children. Today my wife Shradda has made *malpuas* to go with the lemon grass tea."

They ate a plateful of the sweet *malpuas* and drank cups of honey-laden lemon grass tea.

"Gurujee, the boy has brought the book *Avesta*," Yatravalkya handed him the packet.

"He has done great service to humanity, but he has done a wrong for which he should be sorry," the rishi stared at the boy.

"The Captain was a great soul and his sacrifice will not go to waste."

The boy was afraid now. What wrong had he done? "I tried my best to help the Captain," he mumbled.

"It is not about him, dear Sushyo. Your mother had given you a notebook, hadn't she?" the rishi asked.

How do some people know you more than you know yourself?

"Yes, Gurujee, she had," the boy replied sheepishly. 'What wrong have I committed?' he mumbled.

"And have you written a single word in it?" the rishi asked sternly.

"No, Sir... I didn't feel the need to..." the boy stammered he knew something was terribly wrong.

"Is that the way to serve the soul of a woman who sacrificed her life so that you could be alive?" the rishi thundered.

"No, Sir," the boy shivered with fear and remorse.

"Then promise me as a penance you will write down whatever you learn in the journey of life in that little notebook your mother had given to you," the rishi said.

"I will do whatever you ask me to, Gurujee, please forgive me and bless me for my life ahead," the boy was in tears.

"Are you prepared to shoulder some tough responsibilities and not just dream of being a toy maker?" the rishi asked.

The boy nodded in affirmation. He remembered what his mother had told him. When people offer you some responsibility, it is a good omen and it means you have grown in stature. Never ever shy away from responsibilities.

"That is what I expected from the son of Kara Indash," the rishi closed his eyes.

The boy was stunned into silence. He wanted to get up and accost the old rishi but Yatrayamini held his hands. In him seethed anger against his mother for hiding from him his true identity. Who was he?

He wasn't what he had taken himself to be. He was someone else now and not what he had been the past seventeen years. The boy was stumped into deathly silence.

"These are trying times. Soon the news of the son of Emperor Kara taking refuge in the Sapta Sindhu region will reach the ears of Queen Kassandrra and she will attack us to get rid of the sole claimant to the throne of Arianna. She desperately wants the book *Avesta* which will legitimise her rule over the kingdom of Arianna. We have to be prepared," the rishi whispered.

"What needs to be done, Gurujee?" Yatravalkya asked.

"Prepare your people for the great war of righteousness," the rishi replied.

"Oh! Gurujee, they are reluctant to fight and have grown weak by chasing material dreams and they are ready to buy peace by offering doles to the queen," Yatravalkya wailed.

"Teach them the importance of robust health and a calm mind. Teach them that solitude is compulsory and that peace comes at a price. We could be peace loving people but if somebody challenges our freedom, we will strike back," Rishi Angiras thundered. "Get the *sanjivini*, the elixir of eternal life, the magic herb which will cure the sick populace."

He closed his eyes. It was signal that the trio leave him alone to meditate.

Whilst on their way back the boy couldn't hold back his tears. He missed his mother and on learning that she was a victim of the intrigue of the throne and dirty politicking of the palace, he decided to escape from the happenings around him and migrate to the Himalayas.

"You cannot go away," Yatrayamini announced.

"Do you read minds?" he asked morosely.

"I read human beings and their fondness to run way from their problems. You know Sushyo, animals never run away from their problems. They either fight on or die, but we humans have this thing called the *mind* and the mind always has negative energy. It wants us to escape, hide, cry, be sad and bask under the glory of unfulfilled tasks," Yatrayamini explained.

"If not the mind what is it that we should fall back upon?" he asked.

"The Soul of the Universe," she replied.

"How do you know about the Soul of the Universe?" the boy was surprised.

"Because she is the Soul of the Universe… the *Shakti* incarnate…" replied Yatravalkya.

The Flight to Mount Kailasa

They reached the palace late into the night and ate a hurried dinner before retiring to their respective bedrooms.

The boy slept peacefully and dreamt of beautiful gardens, blue lakes, large tracts of flowery earth and lilting music. His soul danced as if he had reached where he wanted to. In his dreams his mother gave him a clue that the Soul of the Universe and the Alchemist of the East were one and the same person.

Early in the morning he went for a walk on the beach of the Parushini river and bathed in the holy waters.

When he came back he found that his luggage had been packed and a bullock cart stood waiting for him.

"We are to leave for Kalrath's gurukul," Yatravalkya announced.

'Father you needn't come, I will get the task done; you have to make sure that people are up to their duties. We need the support of the three chieftains of the Sapta Sindhu Confederacy and it is you who could elicit their willingness to pick up arms," Yatrayamini said.

"Would you manage on your own, dear daughter?" Yatravalkya asked.

"Yes," Yatrayamini replied.

The boy sulked on being ignored.

"Am I in it or not?" He asked.

"You are the chosen one, Sushyo," she whispered. "Let us go."

She was back to her chirpy self.

They reached the gurukul and conveyed the wishes of Rishi Angiras.

"This is an audacious idea," Guru Kalarth shouted in astonishment when Yatrayamini told him that it was imperative to make a flying machine to fetch the *sanjivini* from Mount Kailas and to seek the blessings of Lord Pashupati. "None has made a vimana up till now. We humans cannot fly," he said.

"Why not Gurujee? When we can sail on the dangerous waters and travel miles around the globe, why can't we fly in the air? Aren't winds like water, ever flowing with currents and have different temperatures at different levels?" Yatrayamini was not the one to let go. "Haven't the Chinese mastered the art of flying?" she added.

"They have but then we cannot trust the Chinese. They have money and material well being in their mind. They wouldn't share their secret of flying with us," Kalarth said.

"Can I say anything?" the boy was miffed at being slighted by the two.

"No, you can't. You should listen and learn, and you should know what your role in the scheme of things is," Yatrayamini replied tersely.

And the boy made the first note in his notebook:

One should know what one's role is. He thought for a while and then wrote again.

It feels nice to know about things and about oneself.

"Gurujee, my father has the blessings of Rishi Angiras who has agreed to send Guru Deveshkarma to help us. None can come anywhere close to him when it comes to the fine art of engineering," she continued to pester the guru.

"Why we can get the Chinese to help us out," Sushyo intervened keen to be the part of Project Vimana. It is definitely more exciting than making toys. "After all a *vimana* is a toy," he announced.

Yatarayamini laughed. Kalarth smiled and admired the enthusiasm of the youth.

"Alright, I know a Chinese man named Lao Itsing. He claims to know the secret of flying. I will get him on board."

"Oh Gurudev!" Yatrayamin touched his feet.

The next evening Devshkarma arrived with his nephew Vishwakarma and got down to designing the air machine. Lao Itsing joined the team soon bringing with him the Chinese knowledge of flying. He kept boasting about how the Chinese had flown across the skies a thousand years ago.

Hundreds of bullock carts laden with the metals required for the *vimana* had started rolling on, bringing iron, alumina and a yellow stone ore. Thousands of cotton bales were stocked in the warehouse and the tailoring students of the gurukul were employed to make a huge piece of cloth by spinning together the yarns, weaving it into a mass of cloth and stitching it into a gigantic balloon. But the work of the *vimana* didn't move forward from the pre-design stage. If Deveshkarma made a design, Kalarth would find a fault in its design and its capacity to carry people over long distances and if Kalarth suggested a proto-type then Deveshkarma would point to a technical snag. Lao Itsing, however, enjoyed the hospitality of the gurukul, distancing himself from the clashes of ideas of the two gurus. Exasperated by the ego wars of the two premier designers, the boy lost his cool one day and refused to work or have any further role to play in the making of the air machine. He had seen the unfolding of a mega event in the history of mankind and was over awed by the technological revolution that the Sapta Sindhu had been through. And yet he wasn't satisfied with the recurrent clashes among the learned men. And then there were his questions which pricked him like the stinking nettle shrub. Why he couldn't have been just a shepherd. Just me, my sheep and my pot of gold? He questioned his fate.

If he was the son of Emperor Kara Indash then the throne of Arianna was his for the taking? Who cares about evil Queen Kassandrra?

The boy was murmuring his disapproval when Yatrayamini accosted him and asked him why he was not in the workshop assisting the great gurus.

"Yamini I cannot stand the ego hassles of our gurus. Add to that is the fact that I am nobody in your land. Now that all of you know about my lineage, shouldn't I be given a prominent place in the scheme of things?" he asked haughtily.

"A few weeks ago you wanted to be a humble toy maker and were happy, but now since you have come to know that you could be the inheritor of the throne of Arianna, you have developed a sense of false pride. I ask you is it your achievement that you are born with a silver spoon? Will the queen abdicate her throne in your favour? No my friend, one has to work for one's place in the society. Now your role in the universe is slowly expanding which requires an understanding of the highest order. I see your mind wavering and keeping itself occupied in trivial matters. A little mind and little matters wouldn't take you far," she scolded him in a firm tone.

Indeed she is right, thought the boy. I may be the prince in exile but I am not a ruler as yet. And to be a ruler one has to gain the confidence of the people and of course fight a war. The boy took out his notebook. He didn't want to get reprimanded by Rishi Angiras again.

"Oh! Yamini my mind indeed wanders what should I do?' He wailed.

"I will tell you a story and in it is the clue for you to follow: not so long ago, in our land of seven rivers lived two renowned dancers by the name of Vishi and Nishi. They were the best and enthralled their audience by their dancing prowess. It was impossible to tell who among them the best danseuse was. Remember only one could take the crown of being the best. When the annual dance festival began, Rishi Angiras was called upon to judge the two. The people of Sapta Sindhu thought that this time even the rishi would fail to judge the finesse of the two equally matched dancers. But the rishi had other ideas, so he graced the occasion and garlanded each of the two dancers. Wearing the flowery garland given to them by the holy man the two began their dance on separate stages. Soon a bug emerged from the garland and started buzzing around them. It stung both the dancers. It was Nishi who wailed in pain and forgot to dance as she ran after the bug in anger. But Vishi continued to dance unmindful of the irritation the bug had caused. She was declared the winner."

"Wow!" the boy shouted in delight. *"The winners are not affected by any sort of irritation and distraction,"* he cried. "Indeed Yamini, you are a genius," he smiled.

"Good that you can pick up the clues and move on," she remarked. "And now get back to the work assigned to you and remember that no work is big or small, each one has a value when viewed through the prism of the Soul of the Universe."

Now that is what I want to know – the Soul of the Universe, thought the boy but he was afraid to ask her. It is better I concentrate on the work I have been assigned; at least I will learn a thing or two about the air machine and the dynamics of flying.

Days passed by and the boy immersed himself into the task he was called upon to perform. So for a few days he pounded the silver grey metal like his father had done, flattening the mass into thin sheets. Then he assisted the fabric students in sewing the cotton cloth into a huge balloon. Later he served lunch to the army of workers who worked on the project. He slept with the poor workers and he ate whatever that was given to him without complaining.

One day Deveshkarma, impressed by the boy's diligence, called him and explained the concept of science to him . "Dear son, science is the application of the principles of nature into everyday living making it simple and an untiring task. This increases our efficiency as well. We, the people of the east, have often been eulogised for our advancement in the field of spirituality but we have made giant strides in the field of metallurgy, engineering and medicine too. Soon Charakachary would be here and he will tell you how to keep the mind, the body and the spirit in good health. All one has to do is to stick to the company of the learned – *sangath* – togetherness as we call it; the fine art of learning of the east."

The boy had got his reward for working tirelessly. He smiled on the sheer luck he had had in his encounters with the men who shape the world. In the Land of the Seven Rivers there were many learned men and women. It is where I want to live forever, he thought.

"Could you tell me about the Soul of the Universe?" the boy asked the great engineer.

"It is the machine which unites the millions of universes spread across the *Bhramand* –the Master Universe. It is reflected in the mirrors of our heart." the guru replied and left the boy in his wonderment.

Now this is a new word I have learnt, thought the boy, *the Master Universe*! He noted it down in his notebook.

Before he could fall back on the comforts of getting lost in the ideas his mind gave birth to, he was called by Guru Kalarth.

"Sushyo, come along here and assist me in making these panels for the windows of our machine. Hurry, young man! Are you lost in the world of ideas? Everyone who walks the path has an idea; we call them the idiot idealists," the great artist smiled at his humorous line.

The boy stood up grumpily and did as commanded by his guru. It is tough to live alongside gurus and Sapta Sindhu is full of them, he reflected.

Soon the behemoth machine started taking shape. The boy was wonderstruck, for he had never in his wildest imaginations thought that a flying object could be built and he had often told his fellow workers that it was a flight of fancy and no more.

And now he was being forced to eat his own words! Despite the ego clashes between the various people involved in the project, the work of the *vimana* was never compromised and was slowly but surely culminating into something worthwhile that the world henceforth would remember till eternity.

The boy learnt the minute details of the flying machine from the reticent Deveshkarma, who worked without divulging the details of his next step and without explaining the reasons for his immediate actions.

It was Vishwakarma whom the boy had befriended and the two hit along well, often pointing out a design fault and earning a pat from the gurus.

The air machine was soon a reality!

Ah! The potential of the human mind cannot be underestimated, the boy thought as he stood besides the huge flying machine, his eyes wide with amazement. Indeed if the Lord Ahura is the life giver, we humans are also adept at creating objects which have a life of their own. Now this machine can actually fly.

He knew something in his heart still lay unattended, to which he had not given a thought. A major part of his days were spent in the back breaking work of Project Vimana, but as he lay under the starry night a wish would knock in his heart. The feeling was euphoric and ephemeral. For a few moments he was transferred to a world of immense pleasure and sublime happiness.

The boy hadn't experienced bliss up till now. What is it that is different with me now? Have I changed? Have I let something into my mind that wasn't there a few days ago? The boy raked his brain nights after nights as sleep kept dodging him.

Then one day it dawned on him that in his heart lay a key to the state of *enchantment* that his mother had mentioned to him, when he had asked why she loved him so much. He was strangely happy and yet a feeling of sadness and extreme longing engulfed him. He found the strange mix of joy and sadness a pleasing experience. It was as if he floated along forgetting all about his immediate concerns and happenings around him. Could it be because of *her*? he questioned himself. He had never thought of any girl in such manner. He had only his mother and that was enough. But now, apart from his mother, there was *her*. Yatrayamini! He dreamt of her at nights and sought her company whenever he could. The world he inhabited now was entirely different from the one he had lived up till now. In his new world he had feelings, passions and the magic of love. What was love? Are passions important? he thought as the blood surged through his veins whenever he thought of Yatrayamini.

Tomorrow we are to fly to Mount Kailash, he thought. It is tonight that I have to ask her what she thinks of me, the boy prepared himself to face up to the one who had nestled in his heart like a tiny bird of love.

She was taking her customary evening walk when the boy accosted her.

"Hi… In our country alchemy is the science of making gold," he began the conversation.

"It could be. In Sapta Sindhu we consider it as the art, science and philosophy of a productive and successful living," she said.

"I mean can you really turn lead into gold?" the boy walked besides her, her aura pulling him with a pious force.

"What is gold?" she asked.

"The yellow metal which makes the world go round," the boy smiled.

"Tell me if you are on your death bed, would you take a trip around the world or try to live a little longer? Try to survive?" she asked.

"Why, of course I will try to stay alive," the boy replied.

"And you can have a tablet of gold three times a day and live forever," she laughed.

"I can buy medicines with the gold I have," the boy said.

"Or you can learn the formula of the medicine instead of working shamelessly for gold."

"It could be done. Tell me what the formula of medicine of immortality is?" the boy asked inquisitively.

"The knowledge of the Soul of the Universe," she replied.

Oh! Not again, this soul talk will bore me to death, the boy sulked.

It was at this moment a gong sounded asking them to assemble for the final lecture on flying.

The boy had again forgotten to ask her about the feelings he had developed for her and about the enchantment of the heart, the love for beauty and rising passions. He wanted to hold her in his arms and kiss her. She had left him alone in the throes of his pleasing anxiety.

"Why the hell did I meet you?" he shouted in his agony.

It was an early winter evening. The sun lazed around the mountain ranges, taking its time to come out. A haze hung in the valley below, sending shivering avian creatures in search for their early morning manna. Time stood still for that brief moment.

A wish lay unattended, ensconced in his pearly heart.

Late into the night, Charackacharya who was known as the father of medicine, reached the gurukul. The boy listened intently about the various herbs he talked about. "Gurujee, is love a part of our existence?" the boy asked, deep as he was in his world of love. He had started seeing everything from the point of being in love and seeking the one whom he loved.

"Why not?" the medicine man laughed. "Being in love makes one happy. It purifies the *mann* – the sum total of our feeling, the mirror of our bodies…"

The boy was happy that the learned old man supported him.

"And Gurujee what is *Ayurveda*? I have heard about it in Mesopotamia. My mother always gave me herbs whenever I fell ill."

"Ayurveda is the science of longevity of life. Our life consists of the physical body, the Mann – the one which is full of feelings and the Soul. We have to keep all the three free of all kinds of illnesses then only we can be called healthy. The longer one lives the greater could be his or her achievements,' the guru clarified.

"And do tell me..." the boy wanted to ask but the guru had already left mumbling something.

"Son, learn one thing at a time... mantra by mantra, drink deep, sip by sip. People, who take a large gulp vomit out all the carp," the guru had murmured.

Indeed, the boy thought. I am always in a hurry. My mother was right when she often admonished me for hurrying up things. Are you dissatisfied with your current living that you seek to hurry up? she would ask, for those who think they are wasting their time living in the present and dream of a nonexistent future are always in haste; achievers work slowly, taking their own time and not being pushed around by others or by the circumstances they face. *Each moment we live is priceless and part of the Lord's blessings.* The boy had tears in his eyes as he longed for his mother. To pay homage to her, he made a note of things he had learnt that day.

Early the next morning the boy was at the flying field with his travel kit.

Vishwakarma stood at the doorway of the flying machine, explaining the finer points to the students. He told them how Guru Deveshkarma came up with a *vimana*, which would actually fly to the great Himalayas and could even carry people! The inquisitive pupils asked a barrage of questions which he expertly handled.

"The tube-like structure is the body of the machine and the wings, made of alumina metal are capable of flapping and lifting the tube into air. Then the balloon will carry it with the help of the gases which will be created by burning special compounds which would emit the necessary fumes, filling up the balloon. Lo and behold we will be flying with the air currents!

"Dear students, science does not punish your soul or create an illusion of knowledge but science is a matter of understanding the principles of nature and then applying them in your daily living," he concluded his sermon on the man's first flight. "One day, and mark my words, man will fly to the moon or even to various stars we see in the skies," he claimed much to the delight of the students who clapped and cheered him.

The boy inspected the flying machine with a keen eye.

Its silvery grey wings shone under the sun. The huge white cottony balloon was suspended on yellow ropes tied to the corners of the hollow tube with tiny windows. A huge iron container, hanging just on the mouth of the balloon and filled with red hot coals, threw a gaseous spray which kept the balloon afloat by filling it. Lao Itsing had thrown his magic brick into this fire claiming that the balloon would have a special gaseous substance which would give it power to lift the huge vehicle. A special rite was performed and the school priest broke a coconut, offering the coconut water to the deities and sprinkling a few drops on the machine. Then he drew the signs of swastika and *aum,* on the door of the *vimana.*

They were all set to go, and the priest wished them luck.

Vishwakarma was the chosen one to pilot the *vimana.* The boy sat on the wooden cockpit as his deputy. Two *rakshaks* manned the door. Lao Itsing, Charakacharya, Yatrayamini and Kalarth took their seats in the rear of the air machine.

The jute ropes which tied the *vimana* to the two sal tree trunks were unknotted and the machine slowly took to the air, soaring high into the blue horizon like a huge bird out on its usual flight.

Vishwakarma turned out to be an efficient pilot and a learned teacher, explaining the finer points of flying to the boy who was wonderstruck by flight of the iron and alumina monster.

The green valley below looked like mother earth's robe, and the boy told Vishwakarma so, who laughed aloud and suggested that he should rather see it as a cute girl wearing a green sari. They boy blushed and changed the topic, "Tell me Gurujee, how do we learn the direction in which we have to fly?" he asked.

"My Uncle Deveshkarma and I have followed the stars, night after night and have drawn these," he showed the boy some patterns on a white cloth. "Through these spots marked in blue, we know we are flying over water bodies, the green are, you know what, the forests and fields. The red ones here are the danger zones over which we have to fly cautiously."

"Is it so? And what about the fuel? If we finish our fuel before reaching our summit, then..?" he asked.

"Then my dear, we can fly into the winds and the balloon will float on the higher rarified air, taking us somewhere." Vishwakarma replied.

"You have thought of everything. We should now enjoy the flight. Can I tell these things to our passengers, Gurujee? They must be worried as hell." he asked.

"Go on, the little girl must be afraid of heights," Vishwakarma smiled meaningfully.

"Oh! She is the devil incarnate, " the boy turned crimson.

Does the world know that I am in love? He questioned himself. Does my face reflect the pleasing feelings that reside in my heart? Am I open to all so that all can peep into me and see what I am up to?

He moved carefully; tip toeing to the passenger cabin and found Loa Itsing and Charakacharya in deep confabulations over the qualities of the *sanjivini*. Guru Kalarth peeped through the small widows, trying to make out where the air machine had flown to. Yatrayamini lay on the wooden chair, her eyes closed and her long hair covering her small face. The boy noted how vulnerable she looked, almost like a child needing all the attention in the world. And yet her aura was such that anybody who came near her could feel it; the unseen power. He watched her intently standing by the cabin door when Kalarth noticed him and called him in.

"C'mon young man, how goes the flight?" he asked. "Is the pilot well trained?"

"Yes indeed, Gurudev. We must be over the Suleiman ranges now. Then the great Himalayas beckon u," the boy touched his feet and sat down.

"What is that for?" Kalarth was surprised by the boy's show of reverence.

"As a humble acknowledgement of what you have done for me, I owe you a lot. Who will care of an orphan like me in this big bad world?" he sat down on the guru's knees. "You where there when I had none to support me, I had lost my mother and the Captain died right in front of my eyes," he sobbed.

"You are a good soul, Sushyo. You belong to a well bred clan, my son, and soon you will have a family around you." Kalarth patted the curly hair of the boy.

"It isn't important who I am, but it is you who have made me what I always wanted to be. My dreams were fulfilled at your college, for what I follow now is part of my duty and destiny. You are my real parent, Gurujee," he dried his tears with his tunic.

"Now... now... don't get emotional. I did what I am supposed to do. But what has come of you, young man? Don't be a sissy. Enjoy the flight. Hey...Yamini, look at those beautiful ranges of the Himalayas. Yes... yes... we must be nearing Lord Pashupati's abode. *Jai Pashupati!*" Kalarth shouted and closed his eyes, mumbling a prayer. "Yamini! Wake up, girl. look you friend from Mesopotamia is feeling homesick again," he shook a somnolent Yatrayamini.

"What... what is it?" Yatrayamini woke up with a start.

"Look out for those snow-capped mountains. Aren't they beautiful?" Kalarth asked.

"Yes... they indeed are. Where are we? Have we reached the Mount Kailas?" she asked.

"Ha... ha... ha," the boy suddenly laughed.

"Why do you laugh?" she gazed at the boy.

"We have just begun our journey, little devil of the high mountains; it will be quite a while before we face your Pashupati," the boy teased her.

"Dare you say anything to the lord almighty or else?" she sat upright and challenged him. "Gurujee, tell him to stop teasing me, please," she complained.

"Young guns are booming! I better leave the field for you two," Kalarth excused himself and went into the cockpit to assist Vishwakarma.

"Look what you have done. Now I have to bear you all alone," the boy complained jocosely.

"You better behave yourself. Or is it the height that has got into you?" she asked.

"I think it is the other way round. You were supposed to fear heights."

"No way, I am not afraid of anything. I mean anything," she boasted.

"So you are the *Shakti* – the power?" he asked.

"I am," she replied.

"Then I am the incarnate of Lord Pashupati," he smiled.

"People do not believe in hearsay, so keep your boasting to yourself, Sushyo. But yes, you could be the legendary Sushyont," she suggested. "Only that you have to seriously pursue your duty..."

"But you are truly *Shakti*, that much I can vouch for. It is my belief, my faith and more..." he spoke gravely.

"We are what we are at this moment and no more," she said and made space for him.

*We are what we are at this moment and no more...*he thought as he took his seat next to her.

The evening sun shone over the golden snow-capped mountains. Both sat quietly as the aircraft swayed violently under the influence of the icy gale. Lao Itsing gave a cry and held on to the bamboo handles which were provided in front of every seat.

"Everything is under control, just a gush of the Himalayan winds," Vishwakarma called out from the cockpit. "Hold on to the walls of the flying machine or something, better still catch hold of your travelling companion sitting next to you," he suggested shouting loudly amidst the din of the burning gas stove overhead.

The boy held on to the small windows as the flying machine kept shaking violently. Yatayamini suddenly embraced him and held on to him tightly. The machine flew into a huge mass of dark clouds which had emerged suddenly, striking it at great speed. It jolted the *vimana* and the two fell on the floor rolling towards the door. The two *rakshaks* gave a loud cry and held on to the door knobs. Seeing the two roll towards them, they caught them with the help of their batons.

"It's alright... everything is under control," the boy kept on shouting but he knew that something was terribly wrong. He held Yatrayamini tightly in his arms and struggled to get up on his feet but the violent shaking of the flying machine made it impossible for him to stand still. "Yamini... are you all right?" he asked.

"Never been so well in my life," Yatrayamini teased him as she snuggled against his broad chest.

"You find it funny. We are facing death and you have time to..." he stopped short of saying what he wanted to.

"Nothing will happen to us," she lay calmly in his arms as the flying carrier shook uncontrollably.

Lao Itsing kept shouting something in Chinese and praying with his terracotta beads.

Charakacharya was quiet, holding on tightly to the bamboo handles.

Kalarth and Vishwakarma tried their best to control the swirling machine.

Suddenly a loud bang was heard and the flying machine lurched towards the left, losing height in a free fall.

The Caves of Rudraeeshwar

Yatrayamini found herself among thick bushes of wild flowers with a Himalayan bear staring curiously at her. She could smell the raw breath of the huge animal. It snarled, licked its paw and stared at the girl as if waiting for her to make the first move. She held her breath and lay still like a dead log. The hairy behemoth continued to lick its paw assiduously unmindful of the girl lying in front of it. Occasionally it would growl softly and then resume its work on the paw. Yatrayamini stealthily wriggled deeper into the hedge trying to hide from the black bear. Darkness was fast approaching and she wondered where her co-passengers were. A tinge of worry crossed her mind and she mumbled a goodwill prayer. Night would fall soon making it difficult to search for them, she thought, forgetting her own precarious situation. But the black bear, as if taking a cue or perhaps pitying on the tiny girl, took a giant stride and disappeared into the fast approaching darkness. Yatrayamini heaved a sigh of relief and pulled herself out of her hiding place. It had gone dark, but she could still see a few broken parts of the *vimana* scattered across the vast valley, smoldering. The pieces of metal and wood threw a pale light. She ran downhill towards the wreckage, making her way through the shrubs and boulders when a thorny bush caught her cape, tripping her in the process. She lost her balance and rolled forward, hitting the hard surface with a thud.

"Stay where you are," a voice ordered her in the dark.

She froze. Afar, she heard footsteps approaching her.

"Keep still, Yamini, there is a wolf on the prowl. Lie on the ground and wait for me," she heard a distinct gruff voice.

Sushyo is here! She instantly relaxed.

The boy walked up to the simmering pieces of wood and metal parts of the crashed *vimana* and collected a few of them in a heap with the help of a bamboo pole He managed to light a small fire. Quickly he placed dry twigs, pieces of wood and leaves to keep it going. The boy then shouted about for his fellow flyers.

Yatrayamini could now see his tall figure against the yellow flames.

"Come and fetch me before you sit around the fire to enjoy its warmth," she called out.

"As you command, my queen of crashes and crushes," he shouted in his gayness. He had forgotten all about the near death experience he had had and his heart beat in anticipation of spending a starry night with her, away from the hustle and bustle of relations and duties.

The boy picked a burning log of wood and came towards Yatrayamini.

"Here, climb up a little, towards your left and there you will find what you are looking for," she called out.

"The mishap has indeed opened your mind to the people around you; their needs and wants," he neared her.

"So you are human after all, weak enough to have desires and ..."

"Destinies," he looked down into her eyes.

She held on to his extended hand and sat up with a jerk.

He pulled her up and embraced her.

"What took you so long to..?" she asked coyly.

"Dear girl, we have survived mankind's first air machine crash, defied death and have lost our companions. If some are alive, we have to look for them. I fell at the mouth of this valley; then I searched for the two guards so that we could look for the rest of the party but the two are nowhere to be seen," he let her snuggle against his chest.

"Good that none of them is around," she whispered. "Let us wait for the dawn to break. It will be easier to look for our gurus." She closed her eyes.

"Yes it would be. Are you hungry? I can't be of much help to you, then, but if you want I can arrange for some wild berries," he offered.

"No... no... thank you, I have you. It is cold; let us sit by the fire. One thing is certain though, this isn't Mount Kailas," she said.

"One thing is sure though, these are the Himalayas," he added.

"Why? How are you so sure?" she asked.

"Two things: first the cold and second, we have survived. It indicates the presence of some power who watches over us," he replied.

The two talked of the stars, their childhood, the impending war, snow mountains, watched the stars and prayed for the well being of their fellow travellers. In the wee hours of the morning, tiredness finally got the better of them and they slept next to the safety of the fire, ensconced in each other's warmth. .

When they woke up they found themselves in a vast valley of flowers and herbs. Streams from the glaciers ran downhill in all their glory. Birds had found their way into this wilderness and sang morning ragas. Strange fragrances floated in the air. The duo washed themselves, inhaled the fragrant air and chased butterflies across the flowery grassland. Tiny streams flowing from the hills welcomed them and they drank to their fill. They then decided to look for their journey mates.

Yatrayamini caught the sight of Charakacharaya and yelled at him. The *vaidh* waved to her and showed her some herbs. Guru Kalarth lay on his back with Vishwakarma keeping him company. Yatayamini called out to Sushyo and the two ran towards their travelling buddies who had found a huge boulder to rest under.

"Where did you spend the night? Are you all right? Did you have something to eat?" Yatrayamini threw a barrage of questions at them.

"Calm down, dear daughter. We have survived but I am afraid we lost the two guards. Something hit us when we were crossing the Suleiman ranges and then the wind carried us thus far. It was not a technical snag, remember this. I am sure we were hit by a flying weapon," Vishwakarma spoke agitatedly. "Poor Gurudev Kalarth is hurt. I think he has a broken leg."

"Some kind of black magic of the tribes brought us down. It was... I am sure... sure as hell," Lao shouted in panic.

"Shut up. We will find what we have come for. These are the great Himalayas where the lord resides. I am sure we will find what we are looking for," Charakacharya snubbed the Chinese man.

"But first let me fix Guru Kalarth's leg and bruises. Here, take a few leaves of this herb; it will act as an antiseptic against possible infection. The purple leaves will ease the pain. Chew them and swallow them at one go," he directed as he waved a flower at Yatrayamini.

"What is this for?" she asked.

"To enliven your mood. Just look at it and smell it every now and then. You will feel as if the world belongs to you," the great *vaidh* laughed.

"Sushyo needs it more than I do. He sulked the entire night," she looked at the boy and winked.

"Uggh....I saved you and here you are..." the boy looked the other way.

"I am fine. It is about time we begin our search," Kalarth called out. "But despite all the herbs of this valley I probably won't be able to climb the mountain. You people should move on. I don't want to be a laggard in your quest to find the magical herb."

"No you are not. During our absence, I want you to design a

wooden raft for us from the remains of the wreckage. Loa will be here to assist you," Vishwakarma suggested.

"No way. I am coming too. I want to find the *sanjivini*," Lao cried.

"Of what use is the herb if we all are going to die in this wilderness?" the boy hissed.

"I can manage on my own. Sushyo. Vishwa is right; we need to travel downstream, probably on the rapids of the Himalayan rivers on our homeward journey. Shift me to a safe place and continue with your search." Kalarth said. "Light a fire which will keep me warm and the animals at bay."

"Where do we begin, trapped as we are in this valley? This might just be the end," Lao spoke in a subdued tone.

"Do as I tell you and there is no need to speculate about the end of the world. This world and the many others that are in the universe will never end," Yatrayamini spoke in a cold whisper. She sat in the lotus posture on the green grass and closed her eyes, mumbling prayers.

The boy went about searching for pieces of wood and metal scrap that could come handy in making a raft. He brought them to Vishwakarma who explained the basics of designing a raft to Guru Kalarth.

After completing her meditation, Yatrayamini opened her eyes. She looked up and in a calm voice announced that they were going to climb the glacier at the mouth of the valley, across the alpine forest and glaciers.

"The Lord calls us," she said. "And we have to answer his call. Be prepared for a tough climb on the snow. No harm will come to us, for the Lord guides us. Blessed are we... Hail Lord Rudra!" She closed her eyes, leaving her companions hypnotised by her call.

Meanwhile, Charakacharya made an invigorating drink out of the herbs for his fellow travellers. The boy drank the pleasant tasting drink and felt euphoric. "It is good, real good," he mumbled and wondered at the whole new world that lay bare in front of him. The adventure which was about to unfold kindled in him a desire to be strong and daring. Indeed, life can be lived only when we get rid of pre-conceived notions. I had begun my journey wanting to be a toy maker and now I am up in the famed abode of gods searching for the herb of immortality, he thought.

"That is destiny and I am going to enjoy my life to the fullest," he shouted much to the chagrin of Yatrayamini.

"Time to go," Yatrayamini gave a terse order as she led the boy, Charakachary, Lao Itsing and Vishwakarma to the climb up the steep glacier after crossing the valley of flowers and herbs. It was slow progress as the rarified air made the breathing difficult and the extreme cold made their movements slow and laborious.

"Jai Rudraeeshwar… Jai Rudraeeshwar…" Yatrayamini chanted and the rest chorused as they trudged along to the highest point on earth. They had left the valley and had climbed up the steep the mountains with their dangerous crevices, rough glaciers and slippery boulders.

The evening approached quietly and they decided to camp for the night at a cave shadowed by mountain rocks. The boy prepared a fire of twigs collected by Lao Itsing and the group sat around the yellow flames drying their wet clothing and rough jute shoes. It would also keep the dangerous Great Himalayan Bear at bay, lest he drops by to say hello to Yamini, the boy teased her. He knew that she had developed a fondness of some kind for him and yet he didn't dare to confess his feelings for her. Lao talked about the myth of the Snow Man who, he claimed, was ten feet tall and had huge hands and carried a club in his hands. "We should have brought weapons to defend ourselves," his quavering voice rent the air.

Yatrayamini excused herself and sat in the lotus posture on a boulder near a snow-stream, chanting the Rig Vedic *sholaka* eulogising *Rudra*.

With eyes closed in piety, her aura pulled her travel companions to her. Charakacharya walked up to her and touched her feet. Sushyo and Vishwakarma followed suit.

Lao sat beside her unsure of what to do.

"Sthirebhiraghai pururūpa ughro babhruḥ śukrebhiḥ pipiśehiraṇyaiḥ īśānādasya bhuvanasya bhūrerna vā u yoṣad rudrādasuryam…"

She continued to chant the *Rig Veda sholaka* in praise of Lord Pashupati himself in the avatar of Rudra, the god of thunder and war.

Suddenly a piercing roar of thunder erupted from behind the dark mountains. Brooding clouds suddenly erupted like an impromptu act on the sky-stage.

A streak of lightening hit Yatrayamini, engulfing her in a silvery fire.

The boy was aghast from what he saw. Was this the event the Captain had asked him to look out for? Was she the Alchemist of the East? He had never seen the glory of the god and he thanked the Lord that he was now witnessing this glorious spectacle.

They closed their eyes and folded their hands, mumbling prayers.

The lightening streak continued to fall intermittently on Yatrayamini who bore its fiery brunt with all her might and continued to sit in the *padmaasana* pose. Then it stopped as abruptly as it had begun.

Soon the clouds started building up and it looked like a snow storm was inevitable; ice laden winds blew across, wailing ominously.

A sudden hail shower put out the yellow flames of the fire.

In the ensuing darkness, Lao Itsing lost control over his nerves.

"O Lord! Help me… save me! Oh God of Death… Hark… hark!"

He ran downhill into the vastness of the black valley.

That was the last time Lao would see light.

The boy followed him but gave up the chase when a gust of wind threw him off balance. He fell down with a heavy thud.

"Come back," Yatrayamini thundered. "There is no place for the faithless in these mountains. Let him go as his greed has engulfed him into its unholy bosom. None should ever think of losing faith in the gods if they want to avoid the fate Lao has met." She warned and then closed her eyes, resuming her chanting and repeating the Vedic mantra under her breath.

The storm stopped as suddenly as it had erupted.

It was calm and peaceful now. The stars shone in their silvery splendor. Yatrayamini lay on a huge stone and slept.

Afar, the gurgling of the River Rudradhara added a serene music to the night.

The boy couldn't sleep and kept the fire burning with twigs and dried shrubs which he had found under the huge stones. He wondered about Yatrayamini and the change in her. *Faith needs no questioning and what unfolded was right in front of his eyes;* one which was within the realm of his perception. He had felt the energy around her creep into his very soul, into his being, challenging his existence. Yet he hoped that she would be a little sweet girl, having many joyous days left in her before she settled down into the world of domesticity. He liked her hair and her honest eyes. She had to be taken care of, he concluded. Even if the world looks up to her as its saviour and a source of piousness and strength.

It was a weak sun which welcomed them. Sushyo had caught a wink late at the night and was groggy in the morning. He went to the stream below for a wash where he heard a cry of despair.

"Yatrayamini is nowhere to be seen," Vishwakarma cried as he ran hither and thither in search of the girl.

"She must have gone down to the stream," Charakacharay suggested.

The boy rushed towards them. "What is it Gurudev?" he asked.

"It is Yatrayamini. She… well…er… she had slept under the skies and I was…" Vishwakarma mumbled. "Where has she disappeared?"

"I was awake for most of the night and she was sleeping peacefully... She must be..." the worried boy tried to stay calm.

The three searched for her till the sun was overhead. Panic had gripped them and they shouted about for her in the snow mountains and cascading waterfalls.

Tired and hungry the threesome decided to climb up concluding that she would have logically not gone down to the valley of flowers.

It was a steep climb up the snowy peak replete with danger and death, but they chugged along, holding each other's hands and supporting each other.

As the day neared a tiring end, they decided to catch their breath. The three lay on the snow, their eyes closed from the burden of a hectic day.

Suddenly Sushyo gave a cry pointing towards the mouth of the glacier.

Vishwakarma was astonished by what he saw. Charakacharya closed his eyes and with folded hands prayed.

Just below the snow-capped mountain peak, under the shadow of an *udiyaar* – a cave, a huge shiva-lingam made of snow, shone under the moonlight. On its flanks stood the three snow statues; Nandi – the two horns headed bull, a unicorn with two faces, staring at opposite direction, and the three faced Lord Pashupati.

Yatrayamini lay at the base of the snow *linga*, unconscious.

The boy ran towards her and lifted her in his arms, carrying her to a mountain shed nearby.

He sprinkled a few drops of water on her face and rubbed her palms.

She slowly came to her senses and smiled. "We are finally where we ought to be," she said.

"Where did you disappear and..." the boy asked vaguely not expecting her to answer him.

"I know, my dear, that you have many a questions but I have no answers. Just watch the spectacle of the lord. There stands the *shiva lingam* made of snow and beside it are the deities who serve the lord himself. Pay your obeisance to them. I am tired so let me rest for a while," she closed her eyes.

Under the guidance of Charakachary they offered their prayers to the deities.

"If not to the Mount Kailas, we have reached the ancient snow *linga* of Rudraeeshwar," Charakacharya informed them. "The one which was supposed to have been melted due to the coming of the *Kalyug*. It seems that it has won over the age of evil and stands piously amidst the sinners and the wrongdoers to bless the people who come to it to seek its blessings. It is a testament of triumph of the good over evil. The *sanjivini* will be nearby; it shines in the dark like tiny pearls. We will look for it once Yamini wakes up."

The three sat solemnly under the protection of the great snow *linga*, absorbing the power of Rudra Dev.

"Here, take the *Rudra Prasadam*, a leaf of the *sanjivini....*" Yatrayamini woke them up to the magic of the night. Millions of stars and a full moon shone in its blithe splendour. The snow reflected the milky whiteness lending a mystical aura to the surroundings. A pristine wind blew around them, carrying with it the grace of the lord.

They relished the sweet and sour taste of the leaf of eternal life with piety and expressed gratitude to the lord of the lords, Rudreeshwara.

"If only Lao had been patient and a believer in the lord, then he would have fulfilled his lifetime quest." Vishwakarma observed.

"This world and the many others we seek to explore are not for the faithless and the impatient; and certainly not for the ones who seek greed and are mired in deathly desires." Yamini mumbled. "He had it in his heart to take the lord's benevolence to the markets of Yemen, Jordan, Mesopotamia and certainly to the Mongolian plateau. Let us continue with our search."

Deep into the night, the foursome searched for the *sanjivini*; only the leaves with a fire fly-like seed in between them were the true wonder herb. Charakacharya had directed them to look for it. So they looked for the herb under the stones, near the waterfalls, around the huge snow lingam of Lord Rudra and everywhere they saw the twinkle of the *sanjivini* seeds. At the end of their efforts they had collected only a handful of the magic plant.

"No wonder all magic comes in small measures," Vishwakarma remarked.

"True, Gurujee, but what should be done now?" the boy asked in his quandary.

"Let us make a jute bag, fill it with ice and then place these plants with their roots intact, in it. Protect it with your life," Yatrayamini commanded.

The boy did as he was told. He believed in the magic of beliefs and the twist of fate and *no longer wished to question the lord's actions.* Faith is here to stay in me, he announced gaily.

"We have come this far for these?" Vishwakarma doubted the whole travelling adventure. "How are we going to feed the entire population of Sapta Sindhu with so few a plants?"

"We are taking the roots so that we can transplant them on the ranges of Kirthar and Suleiman Mountains. The leaves will be soaked in the waters of River Parushini overnight. Then a thin paste of the soaked leaves will be made. A few drops of the paste has to be mixed with five pots of water. A wooden ladle of the *sanjivini* water is enough to give the power of eternity and good health to over a hundred people." Charakacharya elaborated the method to take the *sanjivini*.

"It sure packs a punch," the boy commented gaily as he filled a jute bag with ice balls. "Here you are," he offered it to Yatrayamini, who placed the ten plants carefully in between the ice balls.

"Ready to go?"

A smiling Yatrayamini rushed downhill.

"Where to?" Sushyo quizzed.

"Where else?" she smiled.

"Anywhere." he suggested.

Both ran downhill like little children freed from the drudgery of the class room.

Vishwakarma and Charakachary followed them in a slow saunter admiring the enthusiasm of the youth, keen to share their adventure with Guru Kalarth.

Kalarth had readied the raft like canoe which he called *Kottamaran*, despite his injury pestering him to no end. It was a piece of art, with carefully sewn wooden planks tied to long bamboo shafts at the four corners. Two oars were to act as thrusters and as current breakers. A long bamboo pole was to be the controller of the raft.

"I am afraid it cannot carry the four of us," Kalarth said. "I am injured so I will stay back. Soon the shepherds would be here and I will hitch a ride with them," he suggested.

"And I have to search for some rare herbs; I will like to stay in the Himalayan valley for a little longer. Charak, one of my students would be at hand in Harappa to help with the cultivation of *Sanjivini*." Charakacharya added.

"And I would stay back to look after the two giants of Sapta Sindhu," Vishwakarma announced. "Sushyo, do you think you can accompany Yatrayamini in this dangerous journey and ensure the safety of the *sanjivini*?" he asked.

"I can do anything if she is with me," the boy spoke from his heart.

The three gurus wished the adventurers a very best of luck as the two got ready to undertake an arduous and dangerous journey homewards.

Soon the wooden raft was pushed on the rapids of River Rudradhara.

"Do we know the route?" Sushyo questioned and he struggled to control the raft in the roaring white waters. 'Damn, it is exciting!' he mumbled.

"Raft downstream with the help of the river current. This small river meets the larger river Asikini, near the village of Teerraya. You will then enter the river Asikini and row till you reach the small town of Trimmu, where the river Vitasta meets River Asikini. Row further on the Vitasta till you reach Sialahmad, where the river Iravati meets these two rivers. Here you can hire a sailboat and float on the waters of River Parusini till you reach Harappa," Yatrayamini detailed the route of the river journey.

"Quite a journey we have on our hands; a water life for the next few days," Sushyo continued to sway with the wobbly raft. "How do you know all that should be known?" he asked her.

"We are now floating through the Hubra Valley. Soon we will pass through the most dangerous forests where wild animals abound," she informed him.

The raft floated swiftly with the strong currents of the river. The boy had become attuned to the surroundings, and with the help of Yatrayamini, overcame many a dangers they faced in their journey. At many places their raft got stuck between huge boulders. But the boy knew how to tame the rivers and he had the strength to push the huge stones out of their way. As they were crossing the thick jungles of Kashir, a ten-feet long river snake attacked them, but Yatrayamini subdued it with the chanting of mantras.

After overcoming tough and insurmountable conditions, the duo docked on the shore of the river Askini. A flash flood, however, threw them off the course. Their raft was broken and they were waylaid. They walked for many a miles till they were able to reach a hamlet inhabited by the Habra tribes who gave them shelter, food and tended to their wounds. Soon the tribals came to know of their story and the discovery of the caves of Rudraeeshwar. They worshipped them and hailed Yatrayamini as the source of power –the Shakti. The tribal warriors saw to it that they got a sailboat to continue their journey.

"Quite a journey we have had," the boy noted as they relaxed on the comfortable boat floating on the calm waters.

Yatrayamini nodded. She felt tired and wanted to sleep. The boy thought if this was the right time to tell what lay in his heart. But words failed him as Yatrayamini lay with her eyes closed. She looked beautiful and even vulnerable. She ought to be taken care of, the boy concluded and I will do the needful. He noted the feeling to love and care for the woman he wanted to spend the rest of his life with came to him naturally. Perhaps all this is a part of growing up, he thought.

After a few days of travelling they reached the port city of Sailhabad and were relieved to see the humanity and the bustling bazaars. It was pleasantly warm and they changed into light clothes and roamed about the bazaars enjoying the goodies in the colourful markets.

Soon they had boarded a sailboat which would take them to Harappa along River Parushini.

Thousands of white pigeons were fluttering in the skies of Harappa, white strings of cotton tied to their legs. The birds of peace perched on every household of Harappa leaving the people wonderstruck at the spectacle. A large section of the population heaved a sigh of relief thinking that the war had had an early end, before it actually began. Still some hailed Prince Gandhymedes as the avatar of peace and prosperity when they came to know of the prince's efforts towards human bonding.

"*Gandhy... Gandhy... Gandhy...*" They chanted the name of the messiah of peace.

The white skies which welcomed the two adventurers when their boat docked at the ghats of the River Parusini. Piousness lingered in the air. Yatravalkaya was there to receive them along with Mehraj. The boy was pleasantly surprised to see Mehraj and hugged him. "You have grown up to be a strapping young man, Sushyont," Mehraj said. "Now the time has come for you to don the mantle of your legacy," he spoke prophetically.

"I have had enough, Sir. I want to rest," was all that the boy could mumble and handed the jute bag containing the roots of the *sanjivini* to Yatravalkya. "And someone please tell me what these pigeons are doing in the city of Harappa?" he shouted in exasperation.

"Follow me boy," Yatravalkya ordered him.

"Where is Yatrayamini?" the boy asked, looking desperate and regretting the fact that he could have bared his heart when the two of them were alone in the wilderness.

None answered him. It irritated the boy who was used to being alone with Yatrayamini. I have gotten used to her, he confessed to himself.

Perhaps the time hasn't come as yet, he thought. That is what my mother told me; *wait for the right time, for there is always the right time to do or not to do a thing.*

He dutifully followed the chief advisor of the Sapta Sindhu.

Yatravalkya took the boy to his private chamber and offered him a pot full of *soma rasa.* The boy was hesitant. "My mother said that intoxication of any kind clouds clear thinking," he eyed the pot greedily. Damn I need the drink after what I have gone through, he thought.

"We in the Sapta Sindhu believe that after a task is completed successfully one can allow himself a little enjoyment and *soma rasa* is not just a drink for inebriation, it is the drink of the gods and contains the rarest of herbs which add to your vitality and general well being. C'mon, have a sip. If you don't like it you can leave it." Yatravalkya explained.

The boy took a sip and then as if challenging himself placed the pot close to his mouth. He emptied the pot in a jiffy and fell unconscious.

It was late the next day when he woke up and found himself in a lovely silken bed. A lilting music played through the windows and a haze of incense smoke hung around the room. A beautiful maid served him herbal tea.

What happened last night was part of growing up, I suppose, thought the boy. One has to behave as elders do when one in their company. If the old man offers me wine I have to show him I am up to it to digest the drink. Otherwise I would forever be considered a child.

"Time you take a bath in the Great Bath. We have a culture of community bathing. You will not find such thing anywhere in the world. Make it a point to enjoy the uniqueness of the place you visit. Who knows whether you'll visit that place again or not." Yatrayamini entered his room without knocking and kept blabbering. "And wear a clean dress, tidy up your locks and don't look grumpy..."

That is how a woman becomes a woman, when she is in her home, thought the boy. He wanted to pull her to his bed and kiss her.

"Go on... move along. And hurry up..." she threw a cotton towel at him.

Soon he was sitting in Yatravalkya's study listening to what the old man had to say.

"The queen has made her move," he informed the boy. "She knows you are here and she is afraid of your presence. But you are not the only reason that she wants to attack us. She wants to plunder our wealth. She calls us the *swarn pakshi*, a golden bird and has imperial designs; her goal is to set up the greater Greek-dom. She knows our weaknesses, and worst of all, she knows we are faced with a plethora of problems."

"What are those problems which weigh you down, sir?" the boy asked keen to be a part of the solution. It would make *her* happy.

"A great flood can wipe out our civilisation. There can even be an earthquake of huge magnitude. That has always been a fear for us residents of Sapta Sindhu, as the rivers which are our best friends, do turn into our worst foes, annihilating our very existence." Yatravalkya sighed.

"And who are the original inhabitants of this land? The fertility of my people is going down due to high level of salinity in the water and in addition to that, the fact that the immigrants from far off lands are building up conjugal relations with the locals so as to gain permanent citizenship of the Confederacy. Soon we will have a breed of citizens who are aliens with no genetic strength, hybrid bards…"

Yatravalkaya wiped his sweating brow with his saffron tunic and took a deep breath. He was a tall, well built man of seventy seasons, with long silver hair and a silver beard that reached his chest. His ears were pierced and terracotta rings dangled from them.

"Then there is the continuous hankering for various concessions and freebees by the jealous tribes of the mountain ranges of Suleiman, Kirthar and Kaimer, which pose a threat to the very existence of our prosperous land. The seven-tribe URI alliance is threatening an embargo against us. Our spies say that they might start guerilla warfare against us. And there is Dhumbi… the trouble maker par excellence." Yatravalkya slumped on his golden throne.

"You have your plateful, Sir." the boy didn't pay any head to the problems the old man had spoken of. Instead he was dejected by the reaction of the chief advisor. *Damn, he was cribbing and complaining and not listing his problems! That* is the biggest problem –to cry over problems. Is the old man blind to the challenges they bring and the spice they add to life? The boy ignored the continuous hankering of the old and man and walked out on him. He enquired about Yatrayamini and learnt that she had gone to visit her relatives in the nearby village. How could she go away without informing him? The boy was angry. Then one of her attendants told him that the girl went to the village whenever she wanted to take stock of the things. *Take stock of the things.* Now this was a new phrase for him. He never took stock of things. He went about through his chores, listened to people and followed their instructions.

Now is the time, he thought. But how does one take stock of things? he questioned.

The whole day he roamed about in the royal gardens. He longed for Yatrayamini. She had taught him many things and now when he needed her the most, she had just disappeared.

Tired and frustrated the boy locked himself in his room. He sat by the window and then he felt as he had never felt before. He could think for himself. He had to. There was no way out.

A wave of self-realisation swept over him.

I am the rightful heir to the throne of Arianna, my parents were murdered by the evil Queen Kassandrra, I have taken refuge in the land of seven rivers, the citizens of which are themselves deep in trouble.

"And there are no immediate solutions!" the boy shouted.

But if there are problems, there are bound to be solutions, the boy thought. Why, even the medicine man Charakachary had a herb for each ailment. Why, most of them were bitter and unpalatable, but effective.

The boy took out his notebook and listed his achievements:
- He had survived despite facing a near death experience.
- He managed to get into a renowned art college.
- He had mastered the art of toy making.
- He had contributed his bit in making the first flying machine mankind had made.
- He had flown in the first flight of mankind, survived a crash

and tailed Yatrayamini to search for the immortal herb –
sanjivini.

- He had taken the torturous, adventurous route to come back to Harappa.
- He was the Prince of Arianna.
- He had learnt to handle grief.
- He had found masters who had opened his heart and mind to the need to gain wisdom.
- He had fallen in love.

He was happy with his achievements and decided to list his shortcomings:

- He was still full of doubts and feared failures.
- He wanted to hurry up things.
- He was still a novice when it came to dealing with people.
- He feared change the moment a given situation made him happy.
- He was content.
- He feared war.
- He hadn't confessed his love for Yatrayamini as there were knots around him which prevented him from expressing himself.

The boy confabulated with himself and felt better. If he did not have the solutions, he could now at least claim that he was aware of his problems. And he had *taken stock of things*. He laughed and decided to treat himself with a visit to the bazaars and perhaps buy a present for Yatrayamini.

The bazaars were bustling with gaiety. He brought a sugar candy and licked at it. Then he ate some fruits which were being distributed for free and finally bought a garland of terracotta beads. He wanted to buy a pair of metal earrings for Yatrayamini but he didn't have enough coins. It made him aware that money was important and he could be a prince but he was still a pauper! He took a detour and sauntered near the beach. He came across an isolated cottage with a fertile vegetable garden. Tomatoes, cucumber, snake gourd and other assorted vegetables grew along with ripe lemons and grapefruits. He called out to the owner and when no one replied, he decided to help himself with a few cucumbers and lemons. Out came the boy's bag and soon he filled half of it with vegetables and fruits. As he was about to bite into a green cucumber, a deep and gruff voice rent the air. "Hark!" the voice ordered. "You are a thief and you will be punished for pilfering the produce of my garden."

The boy was taken aback but he held on to the bag of vegetables. He looked around. "Who is it?" he asked tentatively. "Come out, I am ready to pay for them," he said sheepishly, for he knew he had done a wrong.

"Do not lie. You are broke, but to hide your one wrong you have committed another sin. You have lied to me," the voice boomed in anger.

"I can rush to the palace and bring the money," the boy boasted thinking that he should let it be known to his accuser that he was well connected.

"Shut up!" The voice was angry. "Why can't you accept your folly and say sorry?"

"I am the Prince of Arianna," the boy played his last dice to save his face.

"Ah! A pauper of a prince without an entourage and without a kingdom!" the voice jeered at him. "Since you are a prince, your punishment would be double of what I had previously thought for you."

Seeing no way out and a crowd building up around him, the boy thought that he should accept whatever punishment the voice gave him and make good his escape from this mess he had landed himself in.

"I had thought that I would ask you five questions and if you answer them correctly you would be let off, but now you will have to answer ten questions. Are you ready?" the voice asked.

"Yes I am." the boy mumbled and prayed.

"Good, here comes my first question but I don't want ambiguous answers. All your answers should be objective and to the point. Who is more important of the parent; a father or a mother?"

The boy was stumped. He hadn't had the privilege of experiencing fatherly affection to the fullest but he knew if he said mother then he was ignoring the one who was responsible for his birth and if he answered both, the answer would be ambiguous. After a brief while he replied. "A mother is weightier than the earth and father is higher than the heavens."

"Good," the voice seemed relenting. "Now for the next question; how does one control the thing which is faster than the wind?"

The boy was stumped again but now he was enjoying the challenge. He sat comfortably on the ground, thought hard and then he replied. "The mind is faster than the wind and it can be controlled by concentrating on the divine."

"Ah! Boy you are smart," the voice shouted gleefully. "But I won't leave you at that. Here comes my next question – what would be that one thing you would want to renounce at this very moment?"

"Pride," the boy answered quickly having experienced its pitfall a few moments ago.

"What is most peaceful experience one can aspire for?" the voice asked.

"The enchantment of the heart... love," the boy replied.

"What is it that one should immediately distance oneself from?"

"Anger," the boy replied.

"What is the real achievement of a man?" the voice asked. "Being merciful," the boy replied. "What is the greatest wonder on earth?" the voice asked.

"One's mother," the boy replied proudly.

"What is the true path for a man?" the voice asked.

"The path which one carves for himself with the help of his gurus, the books of learning and his well wishers," the boy was enjoying this little quiz.

"What is that eternal truth which can never be denied?" the voice asked.

"That there are many a problems in one's life," the boy answered with aplomb.

"Good, my son, here comes my last question and if you answer it you will have the freedom to pluck the vegetables of your choice; what is the greatest form of knowledge?"

"To know one's duty," the boy was relieved and took a deep breath. He had passed this small test and it made him happy.

A pause hung for a while and suddenly an old, shrivelled man with long hair and a thin body smeared with ash emerged from a hole in the earth.

"I am two hundred years old and for last hundred years I had not come out from under the earth. It had been prophesied that when the Prince of Arianna comes and answers my questions, I will be free of the curse that had befallen on me by my guru when I had refused to follow his teachings. Now you have freed me, you can have your share of vegetables from my garden which is tended by the positive powers that reside in me. But do you know what brings you here?" the sadhu asked.

"My greed, perhaps," the boy replied. " I was keen to taste the sweet cucumbers."

"You have forgotten to read the omens," the old man said. "That is what shiny living does. You have let your guard down, now that you know you have the *sanjivini*, you are a prince and you have *her*."

"It isn't true. It is only today that I took stock of things and analysed my shortcomings and my achievements," the boy was surprised at the sadhu's claim about him. "And did you check your pockets? Did you go through all that *she* had told you up in the Himalayas?" the old sadhu asked.

The boy was amazed that the two hundred-year-old man knew everything about him even though he had been in a hole all these years. *He was certainly no ordinary man.*

"Bless me, Gurujee," the boy fell on the sadhu's feet. "Where is it I have made a mistake?" he wailed. "Search your pockets," the old man ordered.

The boy dug deep into his tunic's pocket and pulled out a small, round, shiny steel-grey stone. It was not there in the afternoon, the boy thought. Who gave it to me? Where did it come from? What significance does it have?

"Yatrayamini gave this stone to you when you were in the caves of Rudra. But you ignored what she gave you and what she had to say to you, for you were lost in the glitter of the magic herb – the *sanjinvini*. What a mere stone could do? But my son, this is no ordinary stone; this is the *shaligram*, a part of the Shiva's *linga*. The stone which makes one's dreams a possibility. It is a part of the Lord himself. It is the real Philosopher's Stone, the *Paras Patthar*, the mere touch of which turns anything into gold." The old sadhu closed his eyes and mumbled a prayer.

"Is it so?" The boy could only whisper, over awed as he was by the power of simple things. "I will keep this thing in mind," he promised himself.

"Now go on and pick up your share of vegetables. You have earned it," the old sadhu directed him.

The boy filled his bag and stood in pious attendance. "Can I take your leave now?" he asked. "Now you know what needs to be done, don't you?" the old sadhu asked. "I have to follow my dreams," the boy replied.

"What of your duty? The one you spoke so passionately about just a few minutes ago?"

"The path of my duty is replete with violence and mayhem where I will have to kill or get killed. I hate violence. I am a toy-maker and my aim in life is to spread smiles on the faces of people in the world," the boy replied.

"You are still ignorant, my son. All these years of learning, your mother's guidance, Yatrayamini's faith in you and the trust that the people of Sapta Sindhu and those of Arianna have in you, have been laid to dirt," the old man lamented. "I should have never come out of my hole."

"Why?" the boy asked.

"Because you are still ignorant of real knowledge; the knowledge of Duty and that of *Karma*." the old man sighed.

"What is *karma*?" the boy was inquisitive again. He had learnt a new word. In fact he had learnt many a things that day.

"Doing one's duty without thinking about the fruits of one's labour and without worrying about the consequences of walking on the path assigned to you," the old man replied. "But you needn't worry. You can go back and make toys as we need somebody to do that as well."

And the boy was dumbstruck. He had ignored his own answers which he had given to the queries of the old man! It made him sad and regretful. I am a hypocrite, the boy shouted in his dismay. I profess the very same things which I am afraid to practice myself. I am a false prophet. The boy fell on the ground and cried.

A pause hung in the air for what seemed a long time.

"Now that you have realised your folly, you are as good as new," the old man lay a comforting hand on the boy's shoulders. "Son, there is a chain of coincidence at work and one has to believe in it. War there will be, but it is also a part of the chain of coincidence. So be it. Never fight your destiny. Accept it as a benediction of the gods."

Calm descended on the boy. He stopped crying and got on to his feet.

"I have realised what it takes to be a good human being and not just a winner or a dreamer," the boy announced and touched the old sadhu's feet. "Bless me and I will do as has been ordained by my ancestry, by my teachers and by my elders. I will stand by the region I was born in and will avenge the murder of the one who was responsible for my birth. I owe my mother the blood of her enemies," the boy clenched his fists.

Suddenly there was shower of flowers from the starry sky. A sprinkle of scented water washed the earth where the boy stood. A million lamps burnt for a brief moment blinding the boy. The sonorous sound of flutes created a pleasing symphony. The wide-eyed boy looked towards the unfolding magic and his soul danced to the tune of the heavenly aura.

"These are omens which foretell your victory," the sadhu said. "The Soul of the Universe is at work."

"You have asked me many a questions, can I ask you one? What is the Soul of the Universe?" the boy quizzed.

"Oh! You can ask me a million questions; it is my whim not to answer any of them," the old sadhu winked naughtily at the boy and ran towards the Parushini river. "Hurray…Hurray… it is after a hundred years I am bathing!" the old sadhu's voice trailed the boy as he walked towards the palace.

The boy carried the bag full of vegetables to the kitchen and gave it to the head chef of the palace and proudly announced that he had earned it. He felt better now. A strange peace rested in his soul. He was no longer worried about what to do next. He was aware of the moment and was aware of his duties. All he had to do was to dig up a path and walk on it.

Sometimes digging the path is the toughest part of a journey.

Early the next morning he had gone for his customary walk

in the gardens when he spotted Mehraj waiting for him rather obsequiously. The boy ran up to him and hugged him. "Oh Mehraj! Are the rest of the crew members of our sailboat with you?" he asked. "Oh how I miss my friends," he lamented.

"They will be here soon, my Emperor," Mehraj replied with his head bowed.

"Mehraj... Mehraj... I am no emperor. I am just a boy of eighteen keen to follow his heart and dreams and who has fallen for the forbidden fruit – love," the boy turned red.

"No, my Lord, you are the actual ruler of Arianna; the sole heir to the throne of Kara Indash," Mehraj spoke emphatically.

"Ah! If wishes were horses, we would ride on them, Mehraj. Before I ascend the throne of Arianna we have to fight the bloodiest battle mankind has ever seen. Are we capable of inflicting even minor harm to our enemies?" he laughed hoarsely. "As if ascending the throne is like a game of musical chairs, a matter of chance."

"We are not the least capable of fighting a full scale war, but we are on the path of righteousness," Mehraj replied earnestly.

"Is that enough?" the boy asked.

"Yes." Mehraj replied. "All we have to do is to tell our soul that we fight to uphold the values of truthfulness and justice." Mehraj handed the boy the very sword which the Captain had refused to part with when he was alive and which the boy had forgotten about and left at the art gurukul. It was a shiny scimitar with royal insignia engraved in letters of gold.

I had forgotten all about the sword, the boy thought and as he took it, he felt a sudden surge of blood run through his veins.

"Hail Ahura," he mumbled.

Hail Ahura! A chorus followed and lingered though the air of Harappa, nay throughout the entire lands of Sapta Sindhu.

The Epic Battle

The boy found himself in a piquant position. He had desired the sword but not for leading a battle. It pained him to think that he would have to fight the Greeks to get back what was truly his – the throne of Arianna. He was all for peace of mutual cohabitation, but now, as the war clouds loomed large over the Land of Seven Rivers, he was compelled to think in terms of inflicting losses to his enemies. It surprised him to think that in a world there could be enemies too. Is it important to recognise one's enemies and one's competitors? Why can't humanity bind into a single entity? Essentially all humans are part of the same soul, he reasoned. At least he was thinking in terms of the existence of diverse viewpoints and people who could have evil intention in their hearts. That was what killed my parents, the boy concluded. It was a good thing that Yatrayamini had returned from her longish sojourn in the village. His heart began to beat to the tune of love again. It relieved him of the painful thought of war. Love rules, he smiled at his discovery and went about in search of Yatrayamini. She was busy with her evening prayers when he sat beside her and ate the *prasadam* which was offered to him.

"Where have you been?" the boy fretted.

"I know what you have been up to," she smiled ignoring his

seething anger. "In the last twenty-four hours you have changed," she continued to look doe-eyed at him.

"You're wrong. It took me a few moments to change once I realised that I wouldn't survive if I didn't acknowledge the vicissitudes of life," he smiled.

"That is good news," she laughed teasingly. "You have understood the value of change and adaptability. That's good for you and perhaps good for us all that you are mature and so grown up now."

Change and *adaptability*. The boy made a note of the two words.

"I wanted to tell you that I .." the boy wanted to speak out the wish that lay in his heart but Yatrayamini eyed him with contempt. He knew he had done something wrong. He should be busy thinking about his citizens and all those people who had faith on him, while here he was thinking of an amorous life. That was not his duty; he assured himself and pleaded forgiveness through his expressive eyes.

"Appearances and reality are two different sides of the same coin," she said. "It is up to you to find the difference between the two and live your life according to the knowledge of their degree of difference," she had left him before he could ask what her rebuke was all about.

He sulked through the night. What he saw was what he believed, but was it all about the so-called *reality*? This was a new word for the boy. *Reality*. Aren't things as they appear to the senses of touch, smell, sight, taste and hearing? Or is reality behind all that what passes the test of the senses? Does it mean that the senses are not to be trusted? If not the senses what should one trust? If reality is beyond the senses then it cannot be physical? So the reality is like the soul of the world. It can be a part of the Soul of the Universe. He realised that truth was what one has to experience and not what was supplied from an outside source. I have to experience the truth, he mumbled. It kept him awake late into the night. The entire mansion slept in peaceful bliss and here he was worried about the difference between appearance and reality. He laughed aloud. If it keeps me awake for the night it better be an important question, he thought and took out his notebook in which he had started jotting down his 'discoveries' and in which he 'took stock of things'. In it he wrote down the words 'appearance' and 'reality' in separate pages and then noted down things he felt came under the respective heads.

Appearance	Reality
Painting (he saw)	Beauty (he felt)
Lady (he saw the maid get up for a sip of water)	Mother (his need)
Barking of a dog (he heard)	Keeping a watch (purpose)
Dark skies (he saw outside the window)	Vastness (he felt)
Stars (he saw)	Hope(he felt)
Fear of war (Ah! The sixth sense-mind)	Duty (that was his soul!)
Hope of victory (he desired)	Belief in preparation (he wished)

The list went on and on till it was dawn. A red sun peeped beyond the hills. He was at work and had filled many a pages of his notebook and yet the difference hadn't dawned on him. He was tired and rested his swollen eyes. No sooner had he closed his eyes that things became clearer. Reality is what which reveals on one who is ready to go beyond the appearances. Reality is the *idea*, the *purpose* behind an appearance. He was delighted by his discovery and slept peacefully in the early hours of the dawning day. In reality he knew his soul was at peace with himself as he had learned yet another aspect of the Soul of the Universe. And then he realised that it was *discovery of wisdom* which nourishes the Soul of the Universe.

He was sleeping late into the day when Yatrayamini woke him up and ordered him to get dressed up. She had brought him strange headgear and a flowing tunic. He had a new scabbard in which was placed the Captain's sword.

"There is the Grand Assembly in a few minutes from now. Hurry up and come to the conference room," she left him in a huff.

The boy was floating on cloud nine since his discovery of *reality* and whistled his approval of the grotesque dress. When one had achieved the improbable why should one worry about appearances, he shouted in delight.

He was in the assembly hall in time and found it full to the capacity. There were tribal chiefs, Dravid leaders, the chieftains of the Confederacy, and the heads of the state of the three constituents of the Sapta Sindhu Confederacy: Harappa, Chahunjor Kot and Moheazeddrro. There were priests and merchants who were special invitees. A few newly appointed generals walked about in their arrogance as they knew their utility in the scheme of things that were to take shape in near future. Yatravalkya sat on his golden throne and presided over the meeting. The boy was escorted to a smaller throne and he sat down in his flowing tunic. He felt as if he were a grown up man. These are the men and women who run the world, and now I am one of them, he thought.

Soon the assembly began its proceedings and these men of responsibility and learning began their farce of arriving at a consensus. The three chiefs wanted concessions for themselves, the priest wanted to conduct the *Ashwamedha yagya* – the horse sacrifice – to ward of the evil eye of Queen Kassandrra, the merchants wanted peace at any cost and feared that the war would lower their profits, while the generals complained that they had not enough warriors to fight a battle of such magnitude. The finance managers cried about the shortage of funds and so went on the farcical meeting. The boy couldn't take it any longer and rose to his feet.

"Can I have your attention, please?" the boy's authoritative voice boomed the warring men into submission. "If we can't have a consensus among ourselves we don't need an enemy to fight with, we might as well as cut each other's throat. I offer myself to the Sapta Sindhu people who have been kind to me. Send an emissary to the queen and let her be known that I, Sushyont, the son of Kara Indash is ready to give himself up in return of a promise that the queen wouldn't attack the Land of Seven Rivers. Let her be known that I don't wish to fight and that I am ready to die for the cause of peace."

The assembly was stunned to silence. No one spoke.

It was Yatravalkya who rose and said. "You are our guest, but more than that you are our true saviour. You brought us the *sanjivini*, you helped us find the Rudreeshwara caves and you have instilled in our people that thing called faith. We will not hand you over to the queen. If she wants she will have to fight us and get you."

"Yes, indeed," one of the chieftains cried. A chorus rose suddenly, surprising the boy. They shouted his father's name and hailed his mother. His blood surged to his temple and his eyes were red with anger. "We will have her blood," he shouted and raised his sword.

"Yes we will... we will..." the crowd shouted.

The boy had made it clear that there would be a war before an everlasting peace could be aspired for. A priest stood up and said. "We should send an emissary for peace. Before the war we should make a last ditch effort for peace."

"Indeed," Yatravalkya agreed. "You shall go to the courts of the queen and offer her our hand of friendship," he announced.

"And for the sake of everlasting peace I am ready to forgive her and as a token share of my kingdom, I am ready to settle for only eleven villages, in return for her not attacking the pious land," the boy added. It surprised him that despite the impending war, he was making a genuine effort for peace. Ah! The reality is that we humans seek peace just before war!

So the very next day, the priest took the shortest route through the Bolan passes and carried the message of the boy and the people of Sapta Sindhu.

Yatravalkya called the boy and told him that he had little faith in the queen accepting their offer. "My son, the war is a reality now and we should commence with our preparations earnestly. I don't know anything about the art of warfare, Dhumbi the Dravid guru and my Guru bhai, however knows a lot and is writing *Yuddhsashtra* – a book on the art of warfare. He sought the monarchy form of government and we support the rule of the people –*lok tantra*. He wanted a standing army and had imperial designs quite like the queen. He has been banished from Sapta Sindhu and now, as the spies report, he has managed to woo the disgruntled tribal leaders who are against us. They have announced an embargo of soma leaves and other vegetables and minerals from the mountains."

The boy thought about the problem. He no longer rushed to find solutions but discriminated between appearance and reality. Ah! The power of *discrimination,* the boy smiled and noted the word in his notebook.

"What is it you keep a note of?" Yatravalkaya asked.

"Whenever I learn anything new I make it a point to note it down in my diary," the boy said.

Then he thought hard and said. "It is *ego* that makes you blame the Dravid leader. He may be wrong but we cannot do without him. We need him more than he needs us. I will go to his place of banishment and talk to him. We may have to offer more in return for a smaller dividend. "

It surprised him that he had been using words the meaning of which he didn't know. Perhaps he used them to create an impression about himself! The thought made him sad. I want my *reality* and not my *appearance*, he mumbled.

The next morning the boy woke up with a thumping heart, burning eyes and a parched throat. The rabble rousing and war cry made his blood boil. He seethed with a need to douse the conflagration of revenge that had engulfed him. He wanted to pick up the sword and kill as many Greeks as he could. Ah! The violence, the sheer power to kill and maim, to truncate the journey of life of one's adversary; one is God! He could feel his blood come to boil. In him had developed a sense of utter devilry. He wanted to annihilate his enemies. He sought revenge. It burnt him from inside. He had forgotten all about Yatrayamini and the enchantment of the heart. Love, the soothing balm that he had experienced. Now he wanted blood and gore and the dark forces of evil were his constant companions. He spoke rudely to anyone who dared to go near him. And for many a day he roamed about like a soul possessed with the most abominable stoutheartedness. People avoided him and his attendants feared him.

Even when Yatrayamini called him, he refused to see her.

It was then she called him out with a certain degree of force and scolding.

"What is it, girlie?" the boy spoke brusquely. "Dare you talk to me in that tone," he warned her.

"We are going to take a walk up to the banks of the river Parushini," she replied tersely and walked hurriedly.

With a haughty saunter the boy followed her.

The sun had become stronger and a cool wind blew across the river.

"Why did you bring me here? Can't you see I am busy with the war preparations? I am a man and I have to be busy with battles rather than indulging in silly womanly activities," he rebuked her.

"Shut up. War! Let us see how much venom you have? How much your muscles seethe to take revenge? How much fire can you spew to scald your enemies?" she pointed to a huge man who was walking across the beach. He was dressed up as a wrestler. His well built body glistened under the sun and the smell of mustard oil reeked from him.

"Fight him and show us all your mettle and brouhaha, boy," she challenged him.

The boy was stumped. He realised that to be strong and brave in the thought doesn't really mean that one could be so in reality. The wrestler was a pro and a chill ran down the spine of the boy. But his pride didn't allow him to retrace his steps.

"I will crush him with my arms," he threatened and jumped on the hot sand.

Both faced each other like angry dogs going for the kill with their bare fangs.

The wrestler moved expertly and got hold of the boy's tunic and ripped it off. It instigated the boy who threw himself on the giant. The giant let the boy niggle him and challenged him to do something worthwhile.

"I will kill you, don't you know who I am," the boy shouted. But he knew that he was no match for the huge fighter.

Suddenly the wrestler picked up the boy and threw him on the sands. The boy doubled up with pain.

He collected himself and squeezed the wrestler's neck with his arm. With all his energy the boy moved, embracing the wrestler and squeezed with all his might. He wanted to strangulate the burly wrestler.

The wrestler kept smiling as if a child was tickling him.

Then the giant picked him again and threw him into the cool waters of the river.

"The deed is done, my goddess," the wrestler touched Yatrayamini's feet and went away.

The boy came out of the water feeling ashamed of his defeat. But he felt calm and reposed. All his hatred had been laid to rest. He smiled sheepishly and eyed the girl.

"I needed to see that you exhaust the poison of revenge and hatred that had been burning you like a fatal fever. Now you are free of the grime of ensuing violence. Remember, the war we fight is for righteousness and not for settling historical wrongs and scoring personal goals. When we came back from the Himalayas did you notice thousands of white pigeons flying across the skies of Harappa?" she asked.

"I did and they signify peace," the boy replied.

"Indeed they do and Ghandymedes, one of the brothers of the queen had flown them as emissaries of peace. The people of Arianna had sent white cotton threads to be tied on the wrists by the citizens of Sapta Sindhu as a mark of friendship and brotherhood. It proves that when war is round the corner, peace doesn't lag far behind but walks besides it. Every war is as much about killing as working for peace," she left him pondering.

The boy was tired and bruised, but in him had grown a sense of responsibility and statesmanship. He no longer sought revenge but thought of how he could work for peace, even if he had to fight a battle of the most violent nature.

By evening he had made a note of what he would do to persuade Dhumbi to side with them. Mehraj and a few soldiers were to accompany him to the Dravid guru's mountain of incarceration.

Across the Mula river are situated the Kirthar mountain ranges, isolated from the humanity and the verve of the city life of Harappa.

A flock of sheep ran through the slopes with shepherds in tow, followed by mountain dogs, who barked occasionally to keep the flock together. One of the highest peaks in these ranges is the peak called *Kutte-ji-kabar.*

The group led by the boy began their climb towards this peak on friendly yaks on a narrow trail through a thick forest of tall pine and deodar trees. The wild animals gazed at them without attacking and the birds chirped invitingly. It was in the evening that they reached the green meadows on the slope of the hill. There stood a few wooden huts besides a stream of clear water. The boy dismantled from his yak and enquired about Guru Dhumbi from the *rakshaks* who kept guard. The Dravid guru came out with his wife and son in tow.

"What is it?" he inquired.

"I am the Prince of Arianna," the boy announced. "I have come with a message from your friend Yatravalkya," he said and touched the guru's feet.

"Shoo off boy, I have nothing to do with that man. He is my enemy now," the guru shouted.

"I have a proposal," the boy persisted. "One which will bring the two great men of Sapta Sindhu together once again."

"Who cares?" the Dravid guru ignored him. "I have nothing to do with the happenings in Sapta Sindhu anymore."

"The Queen of Arianna killed my parents and now she threatens to decimate the prosperous Land of the Seven Rivers," the boy said.

"Good, they need to be annihilated. They ignored my pleas to set up a standing army and now they face a war of the most deathly type." the Dravid guru laughed deliriously.

The boy knew he had to pull out a trick or two from his bag of magic. He pulled out his notebook.

"Could you give me your autograph, Gurujee?" he asked. "I have travelled for days to get to you and none would believe me that

I actually met the great Dravid guru. Hence I need to have some proof that I did meet you," he said.

"What is in the book?" the guru asked inquisitively.

"Oh! Nothing that would interest you. Whatever I learn I make a note of it, but now all my knowledge has gone to waste since I have failed to persuade you to help us out. What use is knowledge until it gives one the desired result." the boy bemoaned.

The guru thought for a while and then laughed aloud. "Come inside and have some tea. I know what you mean. You are a smart boy!" he guffawed.

They were made to sit on soft rugs and treated to fresh fruits and herbal tea by Dhumbalini, the guru's wife. Dhumbavast was happy to see a boy of his age and talked incessantly about what he thought of the queen's aggression.

Guru Dhumbi called the boy to his hut and opened up to him. He told him about his conflict with Yatravalkya, the ignorance of the people of Sapta Sindhu when it came to modern governance and the fine art of warfare. The boy listened attentively, without uttering a word.

After hours of discourses and complaining, he could see that the guru was somewhat placated. He felt a sense of achievement and noted in his book: *If we are to work with people, we should be good listeners.*

"What is it you want me to do?" the guru asked.

"I want you to put into practice what you have written in your book, *Yuddhsashtra*," the boy said.

"I haven't completed writing the book," the guru said.

"You haven't fought a war," the boy countered.

"Indeed, my son, you are a man fit to climb to the throne of Arianna. I will send my son Dhumbavast with you. He has been trained and he knows a lot about war formations, the weapons and the training of the soldiers. He is an expert in war planning."

"I am ever indebted to you, Sir," the boy humbly touched the guru's feet. "The coming together of the two great races of the Aryans and the Dravids will strengthen our cause and send a right signal to the people of Sapta Sindhu."

The boy hugged Dhumbavast and directed Mehraj to prepare for the return journey.

The priest had returned from the land of Arianna and informed them that the queen had spurned the offer of peace. As if to rub salt on the wound, the Greek army had started building up a war formation near the lakes into which the River Helmand drained, near the town of Zahbol on the Afghanistan-Arianna border.

It was the end of the rainy season and it would be quite a while before winter would set in. It was the perfect time to commence a battle.

Dhumbavast had got down to training the youth of Sapta Sindhu. The tribal chiefs had a few rounds of talks with Yatravalkya and after earning some concessions, had agreed to fight on behalf of the confederacy. Weapons were being made at a hurriedly set up armory and young men were being recruited extolling the cause of patriotism. The boy had asked Mehraj to look for their companions during the voyage. Soon Mehraj was able to locate them and they readily agreed to stand by their prince. We want to avenge the death of the Captain, they cried.

"We must not lose the desire for peace even if we prepare for the mankind's bloodiest battle," the boy kept reminding his soldiers as he went about overseeing the war preparations.

The boy had forgotten all about the love he had for Yatrayamini. One day he decided to spend a few hours with the girl. He went up to her dwelling and accosted her in her during her archery practice.

"I miss the simplicity with which we lived when the war was nowhere in sight," he whispered. "The bow looks like a peace staff in your hands," he humoured.

"Indeed, if one loses one's innocence there is nothing left which would make one a human," she agreed with him.

"Yes indeed, we cannot be all animal."

It is a new word, *innocence*; the boy noted it down in his book.

"That is what we have to preserve once we are sucked into the mire of daily living," the girl said. "The *maya*..."

"*Maya*!" the boy exclaimed. "And how do we preserve *innocence*?" he asked. "What is this *maya*, some girl or...?" he smiled naughtily.

"*Maya* is one from which we have to keep under our control and not to be bludgeon by it if we are to preserve our innocence. It is the cobweb of unnecessary and leisurely living from which one has to keep a safe distance. *Detachment* from the work we do and the routine we follow and the daily chores we are asked to do, is the way we can be safe from the tentacles of *maya*... the *illusion*," Yatrayamini replied.

The boy noted two new words in his note book. *Detachment and Maya*. He also noted that the more problems he faced, the number of new things he learned increased.

Detachment is the weapon to annihilate maya. He thought for a while then wrote again. *Problems are the blessings of the gods.*

"And how is it possible to remain detached from one's work and from daily living?" he asked.

The girl thought for a while and then said. "There are two ways of being detached; firstly, by forgetting about the fruits of one's labour and secondly, by excelling in one's work. This way you will never let your achievements get into your head and also maintain a high degree of quality in whatever you do."

The boy was back to his notebook. He jotted down the word *quality*.

"And innocence is our enthusiasm for our work, "the girl said as she left the boy.

Ah! Another word. *Enthusiasm*. I better write as much as I can before the war begins, he thought.

"It is time to pick up the sword," Mehraj sounded him out.

Both practiced their swordsmanship late into the evening.

Yatravalkya called both of them for a strategic session and informed them about the progress of the soldiers and the weaponry.

"We have to make a move now. My spies tell me that the queen's army will be led by her brother Zeuxis and one of her cousins, Heroo, of the Sparta army will be beside him leading the phalanx formation of the Greek army."

"This is what I am worried the most about," Mehraj was serious. "The Sparta warriors are feared the world over and their training at *agoge* is the toughest training designed for the soldiers."

"What is *agoge*?" The boy asked.

"It is the gurukul of the people of Sparta and is the school where the soldiers are trained for the toughest conditions in the battlefield. Each senior student is assigned a junior one. It is the responsibility of the senior to train his junior. They do not allow inter-mixing with the fairer sex and all intoxicating substances are banned. The focus is on making a soldier strong and healthy. Extra attention is paid to games and they live a life of a simpleton. It is strenuous training which only a few complete. Heroo mentored Zeuxis in the *agoge*," Mehraj informed the boy.

"That is some practice!" the boy was amazed by what he had heard. There were other people and other civilisations that were keen to work for *quality* and *karma*, he thought.

"Son, the Greek kingdom consists of city states, of which the Athena, Thebes and the Sparta are the major ones. Athena is known for its philosophy and learning, but they are mired into theoretical knowledge and are physically and mentally weak. On the other hand the people of Sparta work out in the open and reserve books only for the men who keep their accounts as for the rest reading books has been banned. The two city-states are always at loggerheads with each other," Yatravalkya added.

"It will be far easier to deal with Athena than with Sparta," the boy concluded and wondered at the Spartan way of life, no books, nature as an ally, sports and health being the primary way of growing along with the simplicity of tastes. They would be tough to beat. He was worried but the next moment he controlled himself and spoke with conviction. "But we shall not fear. I will lead the army and Yatrayamini will be my charioteer. Dhumbavast will be our Commander-in-Chief and you, Sir, will be our Generlissimo," the boy had forgotten that he was just eighteen years old as he gave directions to men who were many years older to him.

He excused himself and searched for Yatrayamini. Only she could clear my doubts, he thought.

Yatrayamini was jogging around the garden when the boy accosted her. "I have a question," he said.

"What else can one expect from a boy who is always in confusion and doubt," she teased him.

The boy sulked but then gathered courage to ask. "I am a young boy and here I am forced to deal with aged men who have years of experience and learning and are well versed with books of wisdom and who practice the lotus posture. How am I to deal with them?"

"Does age defines one's character? Is age the parameter of one's learning? What has age to do with being a leader?" she asked instead. "As for the lotus posture, go ahead who is stopping you from practicing it?"

The boy was thrown into turmoil within.

"How old are you?" he asked her suddenly.

"I am hundreds of years old," she replied nonchalantly as she took deep breaths to relax.

"It is not a joke," the boy was angry. "I mean if you are younger than me, then age is a one big farce but if you are older to me then I should say sorry to all those old men I have rubbed the wrong way," the boy was serious.

"What is it that age?" the girl asked.

"Why, of course the body, the mind and the rest," the boy replied.

"What of the soul?" she asked.

Then the boy realised that in this din of war he had forgotten all about the soul.

"Indeed, *the soul is neither old, nor young, it is ageless*," the boy said. And he was surprised what he had said. He was elated by his own profundity. It was as if the gods had conspired that he be full of wisdom.

He noted down how the universe conspires to make one a knowledgeable person. And that is the real dream come true, the real wealth, and the true goal one should aspire for.

"Now you should write some poems, too," she said joyously.

"I will... but only for you," he blushed and ran away.

There was an innocence in him which had refused to die.

Yatravalkaya had dispatched three units of cavalry to the plains of Helmand where he planned to face the advancing Greek army with its tribal supporters. The strong autumnal sun had dried the marshy lands around the basin of the Helmand river and the autumn brought with it sublime weather as the strong winds had turned into soft cool breezes. So the deserts and plains of Helmand, around the Hamun-i-Helmand Lake in the vicinity of the town of Zabhol, at the borders of Arianna and Sapta-Sindhu would be the best place to confront the Greek soldiers.

The transportation of the troops had begun. Boats on the river Helmand carried many a soldiers. Some rode elephants which the friendly tribes had provided and still some rode bullock carts.

The boy had been allotted a chariot driven by five white horses, specially imported from the Bactrian region. Though he was happy to ride a horse and had fallen in love with the animal, as the time of actual war drew near the boy had strange butterflies in his stomach. He was nervous, irritable and prone to sudden bursts of anger. He couldn't sleep and there was a drastic fall in his appetite. He preferred to stay alone.

Soon he was to travel to the war base at the town of Zahbol. He began to panic. He sought Yatrayamini who was always a picture of serenity.

"I am having this strange feeling in my stomach," he complained.

"Oh! Oh! The man in you cowers now when the enemy is right at our doorstep," she poked him.

"It is no joke; tell me how to get rid of these butterflies in my stomach," the boy complained feebly.

"Why do you want to get rid of it? Why can't you live with strange feelings? Why do you get irritated by such trivial matters? I am afraid you haven't learnt the art of equanimity," she asserted.

"What is this thing called... eq... equa... *equanimity?*" he asked. He was enthusiastic now and wanted to know more about the new word he had learned.

He noticed that *the moment he became enthusiastic, he forgot all about the butterflies in his stomach.* It was only the day before that he had learned about enthusiasm, without knowing what it meant. And here was a new word. He made a mental note of it and waited for her to answer him.

He was surprised to note that he no longer needed to jot down things he learnt in his notebook. He could make a mental note of them and retain them in his memory.

"Equanimity is a form of detachment but while in detachment one has to be isolated from an event or a happening. In case of equanimity one has to be neutral and accept things as they come and let them unfold their effect on oneself," she explained.

Acceptance! Another word. The boy relaxed but still he felt nervous and fidgeted with his sword.

"You are still nervous, do you know why?" she asked.

"I fear the great war, the outcome and even death," the boy replied morosely.

"No, you have a lingering fear because it is the first time you are participating in a war. Remember, if we do anything for the first time, we will be fearful, nervous and circumspect. There will a lot of butterflies in our tiny stomachs and we will have parched throats, croaking voices and palpitation of the hearts," she said.

"Is there no way to treat this horrific disease?" he asked. The *first time blues...* he noted.

"Acceptance," she replied and left him in his befuddlement.

I am a beginner and I might be lucky enough to win the war! He was somewhat placated by the thought that it was his first war and hence he shouldn't be expected to be a perfect warrior and win a war on his own. He *could make mistakes, the first time.* That is how he will learn. And of course he has to *accept* the things that destiny throws on him.

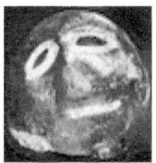

As the Sapta Sindhu army moved forward, various omens were noticed by the boy. Out came rumbling thunder and lightning struck with vehemence. Dark clouds poured heavy rains flooding rivers and streams. The seven rivers changed course and started flowing westwards. Huge storms broke out. All was quiet as soon as the boy's chariot moved. Yatrayamini held the reins and rode in robust glory. Flowers were showered from the skies, scented water was sprinkled and the soldiers claimed that they saw the gods waving at the boy. These omens are good, the priests claimed. It made the soldiers confident of their victory and built up their morale.

River Helmand is the seventh of the seven Sapta-Sindhu rivers; the *Panjnad* and the Sindhu River forming the other six. The holy book of *Avesta* calls Helmand River by the name of *Haetumant* and the *Rig Veda* calls it *Setumanta*. Both names literally mean a river on which many a dams can be build. The river is also called *Haraxvati* in *Avestan* language and the *Saraswati* by the Sanskrit scholars of Sapta-Sindhu and the Ganga basin.

Never had this peaceful region seen any conflict or violence of any kind. The river was the lifeline and irrigated the bread basket of the south-west Sapta-Sidhu region. Though not urban in nature, the village settlements had many important tribes namely; Balouch, Bantali, Afridi, Chikrri and the Pashtoon, residing in them and who cultivated the furnace like flat lands bisected by the great river Helmand and flanked on either side by the lush green vegetation of crops, mainly wheat, coarse grains and maize. Some on the more rebellious tribal farmers grew marijuana and poppy plants for the opiate drugs which they smuggled to the Mediterranean region or to the faraway lands of the Mongolian plateau.

The troops had started arriving on the banks of the river and under the direction of Dhumbavast, the river was dammed at one place to ensure a regular water supply.

Hundreds of soldiers formed the infantry. Weapons were shifted by the river route in huge boats; hundreds of scimitars, javelins, iron swords and axes, spears and a specially designed spear called *sorsa*, which was over twenty feet long and was capable of bringing down the enemies from the elephant top, were brought in. These were the major weapons of the Greeks. Mehraj proclaimed and if they could have them they could counter the soldiers on elephants. Thousands of arrows and hundreds of bows were loaded in bullock carts which made their way to the battlefield. Bamboo pipes and wooden spears formed important weapons, too.

Charak had collected enough medicines, first-aid kits and attendants and he was ready to treat the wounded soldiers. The discovery of the *sanjivini* and the supply of the *soma* leaves had made his work easier.

The Captain's loyal followers had been made the commanders of different units of the army: Meer headed a unit of infantry and he was to be assisted by Russii, Mehraj was to be the commander of the mounted unit and he was to be assisted by Al Fayer.

The Seven Tribes URI Tribal Council formed the flanks of the army. So Pakhta, Alina and Matsya of the Kirthar stock formed the core of the formation because of their inability to withstand heavy attacks; the three Sutean tribe stock, namely, Larla, Hablum and Puzuri Sin were at the forefront of the army formation because of their martial qualities. Lastly the BhutGarh tribes were the suppliers of weapons and were to act as messengers as well.

The four Helmand tribes of Balouch, Afridi, Bantali and Chikkri were given the responsibility of manning the borders of the town of Zahranj where a huge army unit of the Greeks had camped.

At the centre of the army formation was the largest contingent under Sushyont, with Yatrayamini as his charioteer.

A unit of all-woman soldiers called Shakti Vahini was stationed on the right flank.

The war would be an ethical war. Yatravalkaya had claimed and had turned down the proposal of carrying the poisonous snakes captured from the Hindu Kush in little boxes so that they can be let loose on the unsuspecting soldiers. We have to fight our way, Yatra had claimed, refusing to use boiling water and heated oil as a means of weapons to scald the enemy. The use of *vishruses*, *vishacteria* and poisonous insects were banned by the *Rig Veda*, he informed the war council and hence they would not use them. If the the Greek army were to use such unfair means, he asked Charak to be prepared for such unethical attacks and ready the antidote for the soldiers.

Quandhar, a town on the Helmand plains, was to be the main war base.

Ghirrishk was to be the weapons depot.

It was presumed that Dasht-e-margo would be the first target of the enemy army and hence it was there that the army pitched its tents around the desert leaving the area open in front of them. Some of the tents were pitched in the green zone around the river Helmand, too. At the deserted town of Shahr-i-Sohta, the toughest fighters were stationed under Burrannii, who were ready to bear the frontal attack of the Greek army.

Each infantry unit had a flag; thus the Sapta Sindhu units had saffron flags with bold Swastika sign, along with the *aum* sign, whereas the units led by Medes warriors of the Captain had green flags with a pepul tree and a peacock printed on them.

The tribes had the image of their local deities on their respective multicoloured flags.

After the tremendous din of horses neighing, the elephants trumpeting, their riders urging the animals over the noise of the drums, conchs and trumpets and the rolling of the chariots wheels, the night was quieter. The soldiers and the animals rested after the long and arduous journey. Sushyo had personally supervised their diet under the directions of Charak and had given them a pot each of diluted *soma ras*, just to relax them, he had reasoned.

The boy spotted Al Fayer and called him out. "Al Fayer, how goes the preparations of the war?" he asked.

"We have to keep our fingers crossed," the tall fighter replied. "Do you remember under what circumstances we met? There was a time when I had refused to let Mehraj bring you on board the *Gilgamesh*. What use is a corpse? I had asked. You know what he replied? How would you? You were as good as dead. The learned Mehraj said that in times of need one should look to do good deeds so that it becomes imperative for the Lord to return what you have done. The good deeds are the best friends when one is down and out. Mehraj convinced me to pick you up and treat you. I did what he directed little knowing that you were my own blood, one of us, my master. Only if the Captain had been alive, we would have been assured of victory," he wiped a tear and took a deep breath.

Good deeds! The boy sat down and started counting the good deeds he had done. Enough to make the Lord bless me, he mumbled.

"Indeed the Captain could have been of much use but I am as good as him," the boy dared. "You do your best and leave the rest to me."

A loud sound of trumpets surprised them. It was followed by a huge cloud of dust that rose from across the borders in the territory of South Arianna. The sounds of drums rent the air, followed by the neighing of the horses. Heavy footsteps of the soldiers marching shook the ground.

"They are coming… they are coming!" the voice of the messenger filled the air.

'The Greeks have camped across the Lake Hamun-i-Helmand… many of them… countless… sea of fighters… be prepared… be prepared…." warned the messenger.

"We are ready for them… for them…."

A distinct sound rose from the ranks of Sapta Sindhu army.

It was Yatravalkavya who stood on the raised wooden platform and addressed the soldiers.

By the evening, the excitement of war had gripped the war zone of the Helmand region.

Late into the evening a procession of Greek soldiers entered the campsite of the Sapta Sindhu army led by Prince Eleusis.

Yatravalkavya welcomed him to his tent and offered him herbal tea and dates.

He offered the prince a white flag with olive leaves imprinted on it and in all his humility wished them luck for the war.

"I had thought that the sheer size of our army would make you think twice before commencing this war, but… Mehraj… didn't you educate your friends about our edge over the Sapta Sindhu army?" the prince addressed Mehraj.

"On the contrary my friend, I told them about the course that justice takes and how, at the end of it all, the upright and the honest emerge the victors," Mehraj replied.

"You are the same old fighter with the never say die spirit. Save your prince or else he will meet the same fate as your queen and the emperor did," the prince threw a challenge.

"It is supposed to be a war with weapons. Since when have the Greeks started being bombastic, using words as weapons?" Yatravalkaya intervened.

"Since the people of Sapta Sindhu have left weights and measures and have picked up swords and javelins to fight us," the prince replied.

"We agree to the terms of war and expect you to follow what you have laid in this charter of war conditions," Mehraj said tersely.

"We will, but in the heat of the war and violence, nothing can be promised and no one can hold on to the rules and regulations. Since you are new to war, Yatra, I thought it best to educate you about the finer points of wars, hence this meeting. Now we meet in the battlefields brothers, till then…"

Eleusis turned back and rode towards the camps, then returned to face Yatravalkya. "Hand over the boy to me and the holy book *Avesta* and we retrace our steps. No war and we will give you plenty of gold, precious stones…"

"Shut up, Prince, we may be traders but we do not trade friendship," Yatravalkya hissed.

"Then prepare yourself for the dance of death that the Greek army is about to unleash on you," Prince Eleusis kicked his horse and galloped towards the Greek camp.

"The arrogant are the first to bite the dust, Prince. It is an old Greek saying and how perfectly it suits you," Mehraj shouted.

The boy then saw the Greek army and its logical formations, its shiny weapons and the sheer number of the soldiers mounted on horses and elephants. He was amazed at what he saw. The enemy is formidable, he concluded. He took a bamboo pipe and through it viewed the huge Greek army.

The Greek army moved like an immense sea of humanity. Hordes of Medes and Kaassitte tribes had joined them. The Tribal Council which consisted of seventeen tribes had sworn allegiance to the Queen Kassandrra and rode in its mighty splendour.

Iruta, Shulime, Elulumesh and the Ibate hordes of Gutian tribe moved towards the town of Zahbol.

The Tribal warriors of Emgroo and Bantu tribes were stationed at the town of Zahranj on the south east of the province of Dasht-e-Lut. It was the first line of control for the Greek army and would be the one which would lead the attack. It was here that the army would enter the Sapta Sindhu Pradesh. Three Emgroo tribes were stationed to protect the daily provisions of food and medicines.

The war base at the town of Zahbol resembled a huge city of fighters. The armory, barrels of boiling oil, boxes of poisonous scorpions and snakes were placed neatly, ready to be unleashed on the enemy. Prince Hippies was the general of this base. It was on the right flank and was to attack the Sapta Sindhu simultaneously with the main formation on the mouth of Darye-e-Helmand.

Heroo had brought a huge contingent of armed forces from Sparta and stationed them at the outskirts of the town of Zabhol.

Zeuxis was declared as Commander-in-Chief of the entire forces of the Greeks as well as the combined forces of the tribes. Heroo was to be the war consultant of the Greek army.

Queen Kassandrra herself would be at the centre of the army formation protected by her trusted Emgroo and Amazon women fighters.

It was decided that the attack would be carried from the banks of the Humun-i-Helmand lake which would lead the army through the Darya-e-Helmand into the vast fields of the River Helmand Basin. An old town of Shahr-i-Sohta, which was now a ruin, would be taken first and the army would make its base there.

Daasht-e-Margo was the first target of the Greek army followed by Girriisk and then the main city in the Helmand province – Quandhar. The *bad-a-sad-o-bistriz* – a long period of gale and strong winds across the plains of the Helmand region – had passed and the area was calm till the winters.

The combined Greek force resembled a vast ocean of soldiers, from the dark skinned Emgroo and Bantu fighters from the continent of Afrika, to the thousands of tribal fighters of Anatolia, River Danube basin and Lake Wan region. The Greek fighters were distinct as their height and colour of the skin differed from the rest. They carried blue flags on which two swords were imprinted as a cross with olive leaves forming the backdrop. The tribal flags were multicoloured and had imprints of various animals, ranging from lions and yaks to avian creatues like a crow or eagle.

The army was arranged as a semi-circular arc; with the left and right flanks having archers and spearmen. At the centre called phalanx, were the strongest of fighters mounted on horses and mules. On the first line of the concentric arc were the foot soldiers carrying scimitars and javelins. Behind them were the secret soldiers who carried boxes of poisonous snakes. They'd infiltrate the Sapta Sindhu army and let loose deadly snakes on the hapless soldiers. There were huge iron pots of boiling oil which were placed near the Farah river and on the mounts of the river banks. Long iron syringes would be used to spray the boiling oil on the enemy.

Prince Eleusis rode on to inspect the soldiers on his well-built white horse, covered from head to toe in his armour. He carried a huge iron sword which he waved every now and then. He surveyed the army of Sapta Sindhu through a bamboo pipe and laughed hoarsely.

"Have they brought little lambs to fight with us, Minister Jolgee?" he asked his interior minister.

"So it seems. But, Prince, we should never underestimate the enemy," the interior minister replied.

"Is the old fox, Dhumbi, with them?" he asked.

"His son Dhumbavast is present," Jolgee replied.

"Then who is leading the army?"

"The boy. The son of Kara Indash and Queen Leila," the minister replied.

"Ah! The lamb has risen to avenge the death of his shepherd. Let him come and we will help him meet his parents," the prince laughed.

On the outskirts of the town of Zahbol, the Spartan army stood in a phalanx, on the vast grounds, surrounded by a small mountain range on one side and a river stream on the other. The Hoplite soldiers stood in a close phalanx formation; presenting a wall of armour and spear points to the enemy. The shields, also known as *aspris*, were made of wood and bronze and were locked together. The spears called *doru* were held out over the shields. Tall and well built Spartan soldiers wore bronze breast plates and metal greaves over the stiff clothing.

Heroo surveyed the Phalanx formation and smiled.

"Are the *peltasts* – the javelin throwers – ready?" he asked one of his majors.

"Yes, General," the major replied.

"Good. Tell them to take care of the tribal warriors."

"Yes, General. What about the mounted archers?" the major asked.

"Ah! The master archers! The strength of Spartan army… Tell them to hide the sun with their arrows so that the enemy fears our warring ability," Heroo directed the major and kicked his horse, riding through the grounds and climbing the hillock. It is important to create a spectacle in any war as it acts as a deterrent and breaks the spirit of the enemy, thought Heroo. The sheer size and discipline of our army is enough to make the Sapta Sindhu army run away to save their skins.

What the boy thought was different from what he saw – that appearences can be deceptive. The reality can be heartbreaking, he thought. He did not see the huge armies, but the world divided into two opposite camps: the right and the wrong, the good and the evil, the aggressor and the defender, the unrighteous and the righteous, the arrogant and the humble. It is not the people who are inclined to fight against each other but the men who lead them. Humanity as a rule wants to relate with each other and wars are an exception to this rule.

The boy walked slowly up to his chariot and took his seat. He pulled up his coat of mail and checked the weaponry he had. There shone the scimitar of the Captain. It once belonged to his father, the emperor. It must have slain hundreds of fighters. It pained him that he was an inheritor of battles and wars – of violence. If only he could put an end to all this and give the coming generation a legacy of peace and togetherness, the boy thought.

"Ah! A thinker! Boy, your tribe is not required in the battlefield; they say that a thinking man is a failure as a man of action," Yatrayamini confronted the boy in his confab.

"I don't agree to what you say," the boy replied tersely. It surprised him that he could disagree with the one he loved and learnt from. "Until one thinks one cannot act in a proper manner. *Thinking is the oil which lubricates the actions we undertake.*"

"And we have been ignorant of the presence of a savant amongst us," she giggled.

"You never take me seriously," he complained.

"You always take me seriously," she smiled.

"You are just a girl wanting a home and someone to take care of you," the boy said.

"And you are a boy who want to be pampered and encouraged in all for his thoughts and actions," she added.

"All I want is what I can get from you," the boy smiled meaningfully.

"All I can give is what you want from me," she said, turning crimson.

The two stared at each other under the starry sky. A cool breeze blew across the river Helmand. A calm before the storm engulfed their existence. The boy walked up to her and took her in his arms.

"Your eyes are expressive yet they hide a lot," he held her in his arms and then he kissed her.

The next morning, the blowing of the conchs and the trumpets, the beating of the drums and the war cries of the soldiers woke the two up. They found themselves in each other's arms. The boy blushed and arranged his armour. Yatrayamini took hold of the reins of the chariot and cried.

"Jai ho..Rudreeshwar!"

The boy joined her in shouting and praying. The boy's chariot, guided by Yatrayamini rushed towards the enemy line on the Zahranj-Sapta Sindhu borders.

"Do not lose your heart and hope. Keep moving... keep moving..." Yatrayamini shouted.

The war had well and truly begun. It was mayhem and there was blood and gore all around. Men fought like wild animals, ignoring the sensibilities of being humans. Blood flowed freely through the Helmand plains. The earth was littered with body parts; limbs, hands, heads and torsos. The wounded begged to be put to death while the dying prayed for their last rites to be performed for a peaceful journey into other world. Still some begged Yama, the lord of death, to spare them. But the strong and the daring fought unmindful of the hanging spectre of death.

The formidable Greek army was given a taste of its own medicine by the tyro fighters of the Sapta Sindhu, who fought like the possessed souls out to uphold the dignity of their freedom and right to live peacefully. The Greek fighters retaliated in the most frightful and violent manner, as if they had a point to prove that they were the best when it came to killing and maiming their fellow beings.

It was the most hideous spectacle and was certainly not for the faint hearted. The crying and howling of the soldiers attracted wild animals who were keen to nibble on the flesh of the freshly-slain soldiers.

The battle would rage on for many a days. There were many sectors where the fighting was in progress. Though the action was to be only during the daytime, the fighting sometimes stretched into the night as well and the armies fought with the help of the torches made of the bark of pine trees and flares made of cotton rags.

As evening fell the soldiers retired to their respective tents and assessed the losses they had suffered. They relaxed by singing and dancing.

Each day the troop formation was changed. Under the directions of Dhumbavast, the war formation was continuously being upgraded for countering the war formations of the Greek army. So if the Greek army had a fish formation, then Dhumbavast designed the formation of the net, so as to nullify the enemy.

The tribal fighters fought with valour but they needed the guidance of Yatravalkaya. The loyal followers of the late Captain turned out to be the most efficient fighters and inflicted heavy losses on the Greek army. They broke through the phalanx formation and inflicted heavy losses on the Spartan contingent.

Each day there was deathly despair and mournful dejection on the losing side and momentous joys and showy exultation of winning on the other. The Sapta Sindhu army soon realised that they had suffered heavy casualties. A sense of brooding hopelessness hung in the air when the boy got down from his chariot after three days of continuous fighting. He was drenched in the enemy's blood and had killed many soldiers.

"How many have I killed?" he shouted.

"None," Yatrayamini replied calmly. "You haven't killed anyone, you haven't spilled any blood and you haven't rubbed the vermillion off of any married woman's head," she shouted back.

"Whose blood is it then that covers me in a deadly colour like a deathly sheath? Whose limbs lay on my chariot? Whose head is this which dangles on my sword? Why do a million eyes chase me begging for mercy?" the boy cried in his despair, his body shaking in spasms of the most dreadful type.

"No one; have you forgotten the principle of appearance and reality?" she asked calmly.

"Yes, I have forgotten everything I had learnt. My heart fills with regret of the most heinous type; I want to drown myself in the river

Helmand. I have killed my brethren, my fellow human beings. I have sinned," the boy wailed uncontrollably. A fearful spasmodic shiver broke through his body and he fell on the ground writhing with an intense brooding and pain of the most appalling nature.

"Those who side by the unrighteous, by the dishonest and support evil are worst than the evil itself for they are the pall bearers of the devil himself. They are as good as dead. If they survive any longer then they will destroy this beautiful world. Remember even a single fish can contaminate an entire pond," she replied calmly as she got down from the chariot and offered some water to the boy.

He drank a palm full of water and calmed down. The shivering stopped, and the spasms slowly died down.

A pause hung over the battlefield. A terrifying and repelling silence remained suspended over the Helmand region.

"I cannot make out much of what you say. All I know is that I am a murderer and that I will not participate any further in this battle," so saying the boy got up and walked up to the chariot. He picked up his blood drenched scimitar and threw it away.

He stood with a bowed head, ashamed of himself and his actions.

Yatrayamini knew it would take more than mere words to convince the boy to fight and claim what was rightfully his. Death and destruction can shake many a brave fellows, she thought and the boy was still in the learning stage.

She sat in the lotus posture and addressed the boy.

"Dear boy there are some problems which cannot be solved fundamentally but they can only be refined. War is one such solution and to that extent, I agree with you that it should be abhorred, done away with, for it doesn't provide us with a permanent panacea to our ills. What despairs me though, is that you view things from only one perspective – a rather narrow, myopic view at knowing things. There are essentially three ways to look at things; one way is to see a thing in relation to itself, the other way is to see a thing and then compare it to the ideal (the perfect state) and the third way is to see a thing as a part of the grand design in which one unified whole is the only reality. But what do you do? You apply only one line of thought. That is not the correct way. Your way is replete with many dangers and wrong conclusions. You have to apply all the three ways of looking at things and then only can you reach the correct conclusion. So if you look at things from all the three perspectives, you will find that this war you fight was inevitable and a part of the grander design of the all pervading Lord."

Yatrayamini paused for a while and then continued. "Human life is full of pitfalls, perils and paradoxes, and the greatest paradox of human life is that a human being wishes to love and hurt his fellow humans at the same time. Man by nature is aggressive as he was a hunter to begin with; a cave man hunted for food ten thousand years ago and lived a nomadic life. But there were some who desired peace and the quest for peace then represented a valid side of human nature. The problem occurred when the people who desired peace also sought to undertake conquests and entered into armed conflicts of the most violent nature. So humanity is pushed into a state of permanent conflict. Our civilisation is only ten thousand years old and we seek to satisfy our need for peace and war. Is it possible? No. What we have is a state of flux – a state where peace and war exists alongside," she paused for a short while then said. "War is as much a part of us as peace is."

The boy heard her keenly and thought hard.

Yatrayamini continued. "And now listen what I have to say about the concept of duty. You are a born prince and it is the duty of a prince to fight for his people. You have to perform your duty with a sense of detachment and dedicate your actions to the all pervading Spirit. Do not let grief cloud your clear thinking."

"Wait... what is this Spirit?" the boy interrupted her and asked.

"Why, it is same as the Soul of the Universe," she replied.

"And what is the Soul of the Universe?" the boy asked.

"One which absorbs time, space, distance, all beings, friends, foes, relations, humans, animals, all vegetation, the skies, stars, planets, me and you," she replied calmly. "Every activity: birth, death, protection, killing, terror, happiness, grief, joy, comfort, delight, elation, pleasure, sorrow, anguish, unhappiness, worry, misery and so on are all a part of this Soul of the Universe."

"Is love the part of this Soul of the Universe?" the boy asked.

"Indeed it is, for love nourishes the Soul and keeps it alive even when it has to undertake a war like the one you have been fighting now," she replied.

"I think I have understood. War is a minor distraction and is short lived, whereas love is the Soul, and hence immortal," the boy said.

"And I see that you have experienced both intense love and intense hatred. That would make you more of a complete man," she smiled and handed him his scimitar.

"Is there more to learn? I am exhausted. The last few months have been life fast forwarded for me," he held on to the sword.

"My dear boy of busy roads, you have just begun. Wait till you win the throne of Arianna. You will not even have time for me," she was wistful.

"No, Yatrayamini I will always have time for you. All my time is yours. All I am and will be, in this birth and in the rest of the births, I belong to you. All I can offer you as a part of *dakshina*, is I." the boy fell on his knees and bowed his head.

"Are you proposing to me?" she laughed. "Time to fight," she ignored him and climbed the chariot. "Let us go and get them," she said and gave a loud battle cry.

The battle resumed after a break of two days. And this time it was more violent and deadly. The skies were dark for days, hiding the sun. The clouds poured blood and the earth was covered with parts of human bodies; legs, arms, heads rolled along the banks of the river Helmand.

It had been fifteen days and war had broken out at different sectors. It was no longer an organised warfare as in the beginning. Now it was a free for all. The queen did not take to the battlefield but her brothers fought for her. They inflicted heavy losses on the Sapta Sindhu army.

There was no end to the dance of death and destruction. It seemed as if the evil spirit ran amuck on the hapless men who fought the war. Rivers of blood soured high and the water of Helmand River turned red. Slowly the provisions of both the armies started depleting. There was hunger and squalor all around. Epidemics and diseases of the worst kind broke out killing thousands of soldiers from both sides. The wailing and crying of the injured soldiers rent the air. Various scavenging birds hid the sun as they swooned over the dying. The animals from the nearby jungles took to the battlefield feeding on the carcasses of the dead soldiers.

It was a sight the boy had never imagined he would ever see. It shook his faith in humanity and filled him with a sense of remorse and utter sadness. He searched for some solace in his notebook, but found none. He walked up to Yatravalkaya but found him deep under the influence of the delirium of war. Yatrayamini had left him to tend to the wounded soldiers. Both the armies were tired but none wanted to retrace its steps and face the ignominy of a defeat.

The boy searched for his companions of the voyage and found them busy fighting the enemy at various sectors.

He looked for Dhumbavast. He was nowhere to be found.

"Where is my friend Dhumba?" the boy thundered.

An intense search was launched to find the war strategist.

On the third day Dhumbavast was found by Mehraj and brought to the camps, grievously injured.

A team of *vaidacharyas* led by Charak immediately got down reviving him.

The boy left the battlefield to be beside his ailing friend. You will be alright, you will pull through; have faith in the Soul of the Universe. I see a good omen. Look my right eye is fluttering and my right shoulder beats, these are lucky omens, the boy kept murmuring. He made a garland of beads through a black thread. He threaded the *shaligram* stone and tied it on Dhumbavast's arms. "This will keep you alive," he said.

But deep down he knew that the Dravid fighter would need the blessings of the Lord himself if he had to survive.

Yatravalkaya and Yatrayamini joined him in waiting for Dhumbavast to revive.

He gained consciousness the next day only for a brief moment and requested to see the boy, who was immediately summoned to his tent.

"My brother, it seems the battle is over for me," Dhumbavast mumbled weakly. "I gave my best but Zeuxis got the better of me. He has a long spear and a well-trained falcon."

"Nothing can happen to you, this war isn't the end of it all and we might as well retreat to Harappa so that your wounds can be treated properly," the boy spoke agitatedly. "Zeuxis, you have to pay for this…"

"No, my friend, we cannot lose. You've got to try one last time. Get me my goatskin bag." Dhumbavast spoke weakly.

The boy walked up to the supplies tent and brought Dhumba's bag.

Dhumba opened the bag and pulled out three iron rods, no more than the size of an arm, with pointed tips. He handed them to him. "Take these and spray fire on the warriors of the queen. In the dead of the night, throw these rods into the enemy camps and within no time they will be up in flames," so saying Dhumbavast lost consciousness, leaving the boy in the throes of his quandary.

So now it is me versus the Queen Kassandrra's army. The boy saw the way out. The war will never end until... yes... yes! I hold the key.

Did Dhumbavast have something in his mind? Did he give me a hint? If he dies it would be for my cause alone. Every death in this war is a burden on my soul. Why would the Sapta Sindhis be sucked in this mindless violence if not for my cause? Even if they were to defend their lands, they needn't have come so far.

I have to put an end to it all and the three iron rods, filled with a magic substance, could just give us an edge. He paced outside the *vaidhachary's* tent and waited for Dhumba to gain consciousness.

But early in the morning the *vaidh* announced his inability to revive Dhumba. Is he alive? He had asked the *vaidh* but didn't wait for an answer as he rode into the morning haze disappearing in its bosom.

He had decided his next course of action. All he had to do was hoodwink Yatrayamini.

One moonlit night he escaped and ran towards the town of Zabhol where the queen had camped with her battalion of Emgroo and Amazonian soldiers.

It took him a few days to find out the location of the queen's army unit. She was camping on the grounds of the town of Zahbol, surrounded by her trusted Amazon women fighters and Bantu tribal soldiers. The boy searched for an opening into the camps. He had let go of his horse and weapons. All he carried were the three rods, which he had carefully hidden under his raiment and a hunting knife to clear the thick shrubs of the jungles.

It was not difficult to find out the queen's tent. It was a huge, ostentatious and colourful mass of cloth stood at the centre of the war camps.

He waited upon the night to fall and hid in the jungles.

It was a cold night when he made his move. Stealthily he moved towards the tent.

"Hey you!" A guard shouted.

He didn't understand the language but guessed the meaning and nodded his head in an affirmative.

"I say, where are you going? Are you deaf or what?" the guard pestered him.

He stood his ground waiting for the guard to come to him.

He was not alone when he came to check on the boy.

The boy was ready for them. His hands moved swiftly. He hit one of the guards on his neck while the other bore the brunt of his hunting knife.

Three more emerged from the shadows and attacked him.

He wasn't ready this time and they were able to pin him down.

The boy used his hunting knife deftly, injuring one of them in the legs. The second one kicked his face and warm blood oozed out. He struggled to get up but the guards were the well built Emgroo soldiers and were very strong. They began calling out for their fellow soldiers.

There was commotion in the war camp.

The boy pushed his captors with all his strength and ran into the dark forest that lay like a closed cupboard, full of dangers and probable death.

He hid in a jungle cave. He could hear the soldiers searching for him, carrying the *mashals* – the fire torches.

This could be the endgame, the boy thought. Many memories began to swin in his head. Toy making had been fun and teasing Yamini too. Running through the art college and swimming in the Keer stream.. pilfering mother's half baked millet cakes, eyeing uncle Nirroon or pestering father to teach the fine art of metallurgy...."

The rods were cold and unfriendly when he felt them.

Should I or should I not?He contemplated his action.

The voices of the soldiers died down but a wild boar had dropped anchor at the mouth of the cave he hid in. The wild boars can tear one apart but they are not meat eaters.

The boy waited for the boar to go away impatiently.. Morning would bring with it a different and far greater challenge, he thought. Queen Kassandrra's soldiers will be in the jungles. And my own soldiers will be worried about my absence.

Tonight is the night, he mumbled and pulled out his hunting knife.

One swift move and the wild boar lay in a pool of blood, crying hoarsely.

I hate killing. Forgive me Lord, the boy lamented as he ran towards the Greek camps under the darkness of the moonless night.

It was late into the night and the guards had called it a day, sleeping peacefully under the stars.

He tip-toed towards the queen's tent and entered the mammoth cloth structure with stealth of a feline.

A whiff of jasmine fragrance caught him unawares. He stood frozen as the décor of the tent mesmerised him.

"Ah! The hero rises to put an end to the rule of the evil," a sonorous voice guided him to the inner chamber of the tent.

He followed the voice.

On a huge bed lay the queen. A silken robe hung loosely over her slim body. Her long golden brown hair covered her face. She chuckled.

"You can come into my personal makeshift bedroom," she drawled. "To tell you the truth I was expecting you to do something heroic before the war ended."

"Who are you?" he asked just to make sure that the woman who lay on the bed was the queen herself.

"Who would be in a queen's tent... but a queen?" she asked instead.

"I have never seen you," the boy was awe-struck by her beauty and replied sheepishly.

"But I have… you have the eyes of your mother and the face of your father," she went on.

"I bow to you," the boy bowed in respect.

"And the manners of the old Captain," she noted.

"You sure know a lot about my family." The boy eased himself on a rug on the floor.

"Of course. I put an end to it, didn't I? Take a seat, son. You are the heir apparent to the throne of Arianna," she offered him a wooden stool with silken finery resting on it.

"I may have come here like a thief but I have peace in my heart for which I have an offer to make," he sat on the floor instead, declining the offer of the queen.

"Before you make one, would you like a cup of wine? It is the finest on this side of the globe," she stood up and walked up to the wine cabinet and pulled out a wine pot.

"I would like a pot of water instead; your soldiers are blood thirsty," the boy wiped the blood oozing out of his wound on the forehead.

"Let me look at your wound," she moved closer to him and examined the bump and the cut on his forehead. "Let me apply a little wine," she dipped the corner of her robe in her wine glass and dabbed the wound while blowing some air on it. "Does it burn?" she asked.

"No…" he was reticent in his reply as he turned red on being tended upon by the queen.

"You're not talkative, unlike your father. He was a gadfly."

"Was he?" he asked.

"How do you intent to get out of here?" she asked. "Valour is one thing and self preservation is another."

"I have a backup plan."

"So I thought. Do you hear the footsteps?" she asked.

"I wouldn't come underprepared. If I die all die," he pulled out the three rods and brandished them like spears. "Boom… Boom!"

"What are these?" she asked innocently. "Something to blow us all into pieces or..?"

"Something of the sort...fire alarms. Within these tubes reside the Goddess of Fire, of whom you are fond of." he answered.

"You must be having a good cause to take such a risk?"

"I know this battle will never end."

"And our dear prince has taken it upon himself to do the needful. Battles never end, dear son, they never do. They are replaced by far more dangerous and sinister ones," the queen sneered.

"Indeed."

'Speak up, for I see that you have a death wish in your blue eyes."

"Call a ceasefire and let us settle things across the table," he offered.

"We are winning, aren't we?" she asked.

"No one wins a big war," he was categorical. "We aren't losing it either."

"You talk in riddles."

"It is simple, Queen. We go back to our respective countries. I have no charms for the throne you occupy. I am a toy maker."

"Ah! Toy-maker! You have impressed me, son. But what you offer is tardy and cowardly defeat. It wouldn't go down well with Yatravalkaya and your er... with *her*, of whom you are so fond of. You belong to Arianna; don't you want to go back to your roots?" she asked. "Your people, your home, the house of your parents, your ancestors?"

"Being rootless is an adventurous way to live. Queen, you are indeed well informed about my friends and well wishers," the boy had started admiring the charming countenance of the queen. She certainly had a way with men, he smiled.

"The world is getting smaller. Horses, my friend, have made the world a small place to live in. I know all that is why I rule," she laughed. "Wine makes you forget the pains of losing your close ones. Four of my brothers have perished in this war." she became serious all of a sudden. "Son, return me my brothers and I will do whatever you say."

"They have paid for their *karma*." the boy was calm.

"Ah! The thinking young man! Have you read the *Rig Veda*?" she asked.

"Well I did listen to a few discourses by… but I have my own… My notebook is my *Rig Veda*," the boy suddenly remembered his note book and felt better.

"Who is that little girl who possesses the powers of *shakti*?" she suddenly got up to her feet and rushed towards the boy. "She will have to pay for your actions too," she hissed.

"I have these rods, Queen, and they're sufficient to blow out the entire town of Zahbol." He was serious now as he pulled out the three rods and threatened her. "As for the one you ask for, well she is the incarnate of *shakti*. The one which you seek by sucking the blood of innocents. Yes, she is the *Alchemist of the East!*" the boy spoke with passion and then realised that he had spoken from his heart.

"You wouldn't escape alive, either," the queen hissed. "It is *she* who has filled your head with all this rubbish of duty, karma, welfare of the people, need for wisdom, war ethics and the rest. I have an offer for you. Join us and you can be the royal designer at my court," she smiled.

"I have come with a death wish, Queen; there is no going back from my resolve," he warned.

A sudden commotion outside the tent was heard. The footsteps of the soldiers, the clinging of the weapons and the hushed voices of the queen's attendants rent the air. The Greek army had cordoned off the queen's tent as the news of her being kept as a hostage by a fighter from Sapta Sindhu spread around.

Prince Zeuxis himself had rushed to the war camp and oversaw ways to free the queen.

An Emgroo slave of the queen had informed him that the boy carried three iron rods, which, he claimed, could blow out the entire town of Zahbol. A fear had spread among the ranks of the Greek soldiers.

Zeuxis decided to go into the queen's tent to gain a firsthand knowledge of the slave's claim.

"Ah! Brother, welcome the Prince of Arianna; though we meet in not a very friendly situation. He has come for a bargain. Peace or war? The choice rests with us," the queen told her brother about the boy's offer as soon as her brother entered the royal tent.

Zeuxis rushed towards the boy with his spear and threatened him. A huge falcon fluttered its wings ominously as it perched on the broad shoulders of the prince over which shone an iron coat of mail. The boy stood up and pulled out one of the three rods and showed it to him. "This will blow the hell out of you, so beware, and think before you act," he warned.

"Stop it Zeuxis." The queen admonished her brother. "We are no longer kids fighting for spoils. He is right. We need to break this impasse as there seems to be no logical end to this great war. Humanity will remember this war as the greatest and the one which never came to an end. All wars henceforth will be an extension of this war," the queen claimed prophetically.

"Do you believe his hoax, sister? We are about to win this war, dear sister, and the boy has come as a blessing for us," Zeuxis hissed like a trampled snake.

"Yes, I do. He is of blue blood and an artist as well. He wouldn't lie," she cried. "Put down your weapon and welcome an artist. He is a toy maker."

"I haven't yet heard of the discovery of explosives, sister. And why would a toy maker play with fire?" he laughed.

"The boy has an idea for which he has wagered his life and we should respect his foresightedness," she commanded.

"What do you want?" Zeuxis faced the boy. .

"Peace," the boy replied solemnly.

"We will give you peace but not before you to fight for it," Zeuxis said.

"What do you have in mind?" the boy asked.

"You are good with your sword I have heard, but are you good enough to wrestle?" he asked.

"I fought just one wrestling bout and I was defeated well and truly. It wasn't an official bout, though," the boy was honest.

"Let us have one last bout to dissolve the stalemate we all are in," Zeuxis offered.

"If the queen is ready to risk the loss of another of her brothers," the boy countered seeing that Zeuxis was somewhat flustered by his bravery.

"No, don't ask me. For me the best way is to have a peace conclave." Kassandrra replied. "I am tired of this war business. I want to climb up the Himalayas and search for my inner being," she closed her eyes, arresting the tears which had welled up in them.

"No way sister; his coming here and threatening you has made it personal. Let us have a fight to the finish. Let the throne of Arianna be the trophy. The winner takes it all."

"I am ready, Zeuxis. But if you lose…"

"I won't live a moment of a borrowed life," Zeuxis stated. "On the third day from now, early in the morning we will have…. er… what your people at the Sindhu valley call… yes… yes… a *mall-yudh*."

"So be it," the boy said.

"So be it." the queen repeated after him as if putting a seal of approval on her defeat. She placed the pot of wine delicately on her lips and gulped down the drink. In her inebriation she laughed in a manner as if she knew the outcome of the war.

The End Game

A ceasefire was announced by the both the warring armies and each of them collected their injured soldiers. A search began for those who were untraceable.

Mehraj was injured and yet made it a point to guide Sushyo in the art of wrestling.

Dhumbavast was recuperating very slowly and the *vaidh* advised him to be shifted to the town of Quandhar so that he could recuperate.

Yatravalkaya proposed to meet the queen and request her to cancel the wrestling bout. "I cannot put on wager the life of my son," he wailed. "How will I face up to the Captain?"

"I know you are worried about my safety but this was the only way. Either I could have used the explosives in the iron rods and created havoc from which none of us could have survived or...." the boy told him defiantly.

"So you want to sacrifice yourself...or what?" Yatra nodded in his dismay.

"Tell me if there is any other way, Yatra Uncle, and I will listen to you. No, we have no choice. If the queen let me go, it was because she knew that this was the only way. Things are no longer under her control. Zeuxis seeks revenge and it is I he wants dead. Why should the rest pay a price?" he said.

"Baba, Sushyo has an outside chance to win," Yatrayamini had entered the tent unnoticed and whispered. "He has the beginner's luck on his side and then Mehraj is there to train him. He also has the blessings of the people of Sapta Sindhu."

"Zeuxis is an old fox. His companion Heroo has been killed in the war and he seeks revenge. He will come hard at Sushyo," Yatravalkya said gravely.

"I know that it is the duty of a prince to fight for his kingdom. It is Sushyont's kingdom that is at stake. We can merely be spectators," Yatrayamini stated in a matter of fact tone.

"Wars are won by heroes," Yatravalkaya whispered. "Does the boy have it in him to be one?"

"We will soon find out if we have one amongst us or not." Yatrayamini added.

The evening appeared suddenly like an unexpected guest. Two days had passed and the boy practiced hard, kept the butterflies in his stomach under control. He referred to his notebook time and again and sought Yatrayamini's advice about the new moves he could use against Zeuxis.

"Listen to me, Sushyo, it is a fallen benediction on us that you have got a chance to face the enemy. Wrestling is a pious fight in which one is constantly hugging his enemy and feeling him. Remember touch is still the most important of our gesture of care. Now defeat him, but don't kill him. It will set a precedence that if the war is inevitable then one should have a face to face combat without involving hapless and innocent fighters," she left him to find his own path.

On the night before the wrestling bout, a huge fire was lit at the camps of the Sapta Sindhu army.

The boy sat near it, deep in contemplation. He stared at the yellow flames.

Yatrayamini joined him, wrapped in a rough shawl with her hair let down over her shoulders.

"You should have one of those silken dresses that the queen wears," the boy smiled.

"Oh! So you are impressed by her sartorial sense?" she asked.

"She is still beautiful, even after... Why didn't she marry?" he quizzed.

"May be she loved your father, the emperor," she guessed.

"The affairs of the state are cruel indeed."

"War, perhaps, or age.? She has lived a wild life – wine, men along with the conspiracies of royal living."

"Both. She seems to be exhausted by all of this. She has let go of things. Zeuxis will be the next emperor if I lose," he said.

"Could you lose?" she asked wistfully.

"I may win," he speculated.

Both laughed loudly.

"Silly, you might die," she was serious now.

"Would you regret my not dying?" he asked.

"Shut up. I will regret your dying," she admonished him.

"My win will take me far away from you."

"So would your death."

"Yes. Would you be shifting to the east towards the Ganga basin after the war?"

'Yes, if the queen lets us live." she replied. "Would you come?"

"I may."

"Do you seek revenge for your parents' murder?" she asked.

"No, all I seek is peace," he was categorical.

"We can still use Uncle Dhumbi's weapon?" she suggested.

"And annihilate humanity from earth? It is a good deterrent, Yamini, but I would rather sacrifice my life than be cursed to use a weapon which my coming generations would rile me for," he closed his eyes.

"Will you come to the city of Susa?" he asked.

"For that you will have to win the bout," she smiled.

"To take you to the city of Susa, I will have to win this bout," he was as still as a boat which had finally dropped anchor after a tumultuous and arduous journey.

The two were silent. The fire crackled, hissed and sprayed sparks like tiny stars on their saunter towards the earth.

"It is cold, Sushyo. Take this and cover your head," she broke the silence and offered him her shawl.

"Once a woman, always a mother. Tomorrow may be the last day I breathe, let us be ourselves tonight," he took the shawl and covered his head. "You look beautiful, now." he smiled. "Aren't you cold?"

"Won't you sleep?" she asked instead. "That shawl is for the dew," she clarified. "I will manage, don't worry."

The two sat around the fire till the wee hours of the morning.

***

As the sun began to rise on the fateful day, Sushyo stood up and offered prayers to the sun god.

"It's time, Mehraj announced. "Get ready, master. One final thrust for victory and we are home," he said.

Sushyont combed his long red hair, and tied a pony tail with a red thread. He looked a rugged, aggressive and an aged man now, he told himself as he looked into the mirror. The heart is the truest mirror and the boy acknowledged that the past one year had changed him. It had altered his thoughts, shaped his destiny and had helped him pursue and achieve his dream of being a toy maker. There were losses and gains, the boy sighed. He rubbed some mustard oil on his body and did some yogic exercises. Among his accessories, he searched for a saffron loincloth and tied it on his girdle. He tapped the tattoo of the three headed Shiva on his chest. That was Yatrayamini's art, he smiled. He kissed his amulet, closing his eyes in a silent prayer to his mother.

"Are you ready?" Mehraj called out.

"Yes, will be with you in a jiffy," the boy emerged from the tent, glowing in his ardour.

"I will be your charioteer today. Come let us take the blessings of the old man."

Both rode up to the tent of Yatravalkaya and were surprised to find that he was all primed up for the wrestling show.

"I am coming to bless you, Sushyo," he announced and told them to ride on.

Yatrayamini was waiting for them when they reached the wrestling arena.

Mehraj excused himself and went up to the queen's entourage to lay down the rules of the bout.

Meanwhile, the boy sat on a specially anointed seat waiting for Zeuxis to emerge from his tent.

"If you want we could call off the bout." Kassandrra welcomed Mehraj and teased him.

"Let me know about the rules and regulations to be followed during the bout," Mehraj spoke rudely to the queen.

"It is freestyle wrestling, ending only when one of the fighters dies. Each goes for the kill. No rounds, no rules; one death ends the bout," the queen slurred. She had her wine cup in her hand.

"We all are brothers somehow, related to one and all. If your brother dies we will be very sorry so do accept our condolences beforehand," Mehraj turned back and walked up to Sushyo.

He laid a comforting hand on the boy's shoulders and said.

"This is a war too, Sushyo, go for the kill, even if you don't want to. If you hesitate then it will be the last time you breathe."

"It will be easy to get killed. Take care of people who I leave behind, Mehraj, you are the father I never had," the boy was sad.

"Sushyo, this is no time to be morose," Yatravalkaya shouted. "Your mother's blessings are with you. You will emerge the winner."

"I will be a loser even if I kill Zeuxis. But it is true, my mother has never left me. She blesses me whenever I am in doubt," the boy walked up to the old man and sought his blessings.

"*Vijai Bhav.* Be a winner," Yatravalkya blessed him. "Lord Pashupati will be with you."

"Sushyo, do you remember under what circumstances we met the first time? When you refused to yield ground to me and my friends?" Yatrayamini asked the boy.

"Yes I do, quite a bevy of cacophonous girls you had for friends," he smiled.

"Don't yield him an inch," Yatrayamini spoke sharply. "One has to put to an end certain tumors of the past, so as to begin anew. Zeuxis is your... he killed your grandfather, our beloved Captain," she hissed.

A gong was sounded signalling the commencement of the bout.

On the right side of the wrestling arena sat the soldiers of Sapta Sindhu, seated under colourful canopies.

On the left was the queen in her regal attire sitting on her golden throne. Hippias sat beside her. The Greek soldiers stood behind them, cheering their prince.

The referee, an Emgroo major, whistled as the two wrestlers jumped into the wrestling rink, which was made up of damp mud, sprayed with water.

He introduced the two wrestles to the audience and asked both of them to shake hands.

"Boy, wish your dear ones a final good bye. Going by the looks of it, there are many of your admirers," Zeuxis chided the young man.

'There will be more, Prince, once I win this bout," the boy replied calmly.

"Let the bout begin!" the referee gave the go ahead signal.

The crowd suddenly grew quiet. A palpable tension seethed in the air.

In the deathly silence, Yartayamini's voice echoed through the fields, the valleys and the mountains of Zahbol.

"Jai Rudraeeshwar!" she shouted.

The wind blew a cloud of dust blinding all. It was followed by thunder and a streak of white lightening as a dark cloud hid the sun.

Only for a moment though, for a deathly calm fell on the wrestling arena, as the cloud disappeared as suddenly as it had appeared.

Zeuxis was the first to make a move. He sprang high in the air and slapped both the ears of Sushyo with his open palms. A shrill sound of bell claps was heard and the boy fell on to the ground in a daze. Momentarily he went deaf.

Zeuxis saw his opportunity and moved in for the kill. He jumped over Sushyo, bringing down his entire body weight on the hapless boy. The boy winced under his adversary's weight. A wave of immense pain passed through his face and he cried.

Queen Kassandrra stood from her throne and clapped in delight. Zeuxis waved to the cheering Greek soldiers as he stood up, dusting himself and jogging across the wrestling rink.

The boy lay on the ground breathing heavily and trying to clear his head; his body ached under the manoeuver of his opponent. With a mighty effort he strutted to his feet, wiping the blood that oozed from his battered face. He took a deep breath, calming his nerves. He knew that he was against a pro and it would take more than good luck to defeat his worthy opponent. In a swift move, which Zeuxis could have never imagined the boy to be capable of; he jumped on a sloppy Zeuxis and crossed his torso with his hands, pinning him down on to the floor. The boy continued to hold Zeuxis down, whose face was buried in the wet mud, suffocating him. Zeuxis flapped his feet and hands like a dying bird.

A deathly silence fell across the arena.

"C'mon, Sushyo, kill him," Mehraj shouted in unbridled joy.

As if to free himself, Zeuxis, in a last effort to save his life, caught hold of Sushyo's hands and tried to untangle the vice-like grip of the boy.

The boy continued to pin him down with all his might. Suddenly Zeuxis was able to free one of his hands and threw a ball of wet mud on the face of the boy, who let go of his grip over Zeuxis's torso and fell on to the wrestling floor.

Zeuxis stood up and attacked the boy like a trampled serpent. He put the boy on a face-lock and lifted him high with his powerful hands and then brought him down on his head. It left the boy with a spinning head. He lay flat on the floor of the rink gasping for breath.

Zeuxis walked up to the end of the wrestling rink and ran towards his opponent and jumped over him with all his might. In the nick of time the boy moved away saving himself from the impact of Zeuxis's body weight. The boy then stood up on his feet and jogged across the arena trying to warm himself for his next move.

Zeuxis got up and cursed himself for missing the kill blow. He looked into the boy's eyes and smiled. "I have you, Sushyo," he shouted.

"I was thinking along the same lines, dear brother," the boy replied, staring at his opponent with blood red eyes. .

So saying he attacked Zeuxis, catching him by the scruff of his neck and lifting him off the ground. He brought him down on the floor with a thud.

The crowd clapped hard.

Zeuxis was visibly angry. He got up and with a swift movement lifted Sushyo in his arms and went down to the floor. He hit the ground on his back and Sushyo fell on his face with a thud. Zeuxis rode on him and punched his back repeatedly, till he could sense the body of the boy going limp. A pool of blood oozed out near the lifeless body of the boy.

The boy lay like a dead man for a while and the Greek soldiers sensing victory for their prince cheered him on.

'Kill... Kill... Kill..." they choroused.

Sushyont lay still, in a pool of drying blood. Overhead, the falcon piped in joy and with the expectant reward of fresh flesh killed by its master.

"Should we throw in the towel?" Al Fayer whispered. "He might kill the boy."

"No, it is fight to the finish," Mehraj answered vaguely. "This isn't the end."

Zeuxis danced wildly as he ran around the wrestling rink waving to the crowd and beating his broad, hairy chest with his bare hands. The falcon flew overhead, piping in the macabre sound of death.

"Leave him to face his defeat," Prince Hippias shouted to his brother.

Zeuxis ignored the pleas and closed it on his opponent, going for the kill.

He felt the lifeless body of Sushyo and then kicked it hard. "Boy, get up, stay alive for a while and stare at your defeat. Oh Heroo! I have had my revenge. Here lies the son of Kara Indash and Leila waiting for his death. I have annihiliated the entire Medean family. I am the world beater, the *Vishwavijeta!*" Zeuxis continued to beat his hairy chest like a man possessed. "Greekdom is the new world order," he shouted.

"Get up, you son of Kara Indash. Your death would put an end to this game of thrones. My sister will rule your country and then it will pass on to our heirs," he boasted.

"You wouldn't have any, Zeuxis. I doubt your manliness and as for your sister; she is a many-men woman," the boy mumbled under his breath.

Zeuxis heard him though. He stared at the lifeless figure lying on the mud, bleeding profusely.

He didn't have to check twice for any signs of life in Sushyo. The boy, in a sudden movement rose to his feet and with a smooth action lifted Zeuxis off his feet and brought him down on his knee. Zeuxis backbone hit the strong thighs of the boy.

A sound of a twig being broken was heard by Queen Kassandrra. Yatrayamini heard it too.

For Zeuxis it was the last sound he would hear in his life.

Sushyont kept the limp body on his right knee.

He hugged Zeuxis and whispered in his ears. "This is what I had in mind, Prince; sleep without dying, sleep a sleep of death."

Skywards, the falcon cried in anguish and circled over the boy. It hadn't taken kindly to his master being fatally injured. Mehraj brought the boy his bow and an arrow. "Don't look towards the bird, its eyes can hypnotise the most expert of warriors," he said as he asked a soldier to place a pot of water before him. "It is the reflection you have to look at. Then aim at its heart," he directed the boy.

The falcon darted towards him but the boy was swift, his arrow piercing the heart of the bird before its poisonous claws could slash his skin.

Epilogue

The coronation of Emperor Sushyont was a smooth affair. The city of Susa was decked up like a bride. Many Medes tribal leaders joined the alliance floated by the boy and blessed him, vowing to work for peace and brotherhood amongst themselves. A few Gutien tribes also supported the boy's efforts towards peace.

The boy appointed Prince Ghandymedes as the minister of peace and togetherness in his council of ministers.

As a sign of things to come, the boy pardoned the queen and her surviving brother Hippias and allowed them to take refuge in the Himalayas, where the queen desired to spend the rest of her life and seek the forgiveness of the lord.

The boy got down to working for the welfare of the people. For a year he worked tirelessly, improving the standard of living of the populace and establishing a kingdom of righteousness and benevolence.

Ah! The work of the kingdom never ends, he thought one day and decided to undertake a journey to the city of Nineveh.

A three-day boat ride took him to the city of his childhood. Nothing had changed there, he reflected as he sat on the mounds of sprayed bricks on the banks of river Tigris.

He remembered his mother, the childhood pranks he played on her, and his insistence on becoming a toy maker of some repute.

Now I am a real toy maker, I give shape to people's destinies, mould them into better persons, give wings to their dreams and make them smile even when they face adversity. He took out his note book to ponder over what he had learnt and achieved. Empty pages stared at his face! Every single word he had written had been erased. It was a sign that he begin anew.

He sat contemplating when suddenly a whiff of the wind carried her scent. Faraway a flute played her tune and the wind patted his cheeks as if she were kissing him.

"Yatrayamini, I am coming," the boy shouted as he ran over the bricks, his heart becoming one with the Soul of the Universe.